SEPTIMUS AND THE DANEDYKE MYSTERY

STEPHEN CHANCE

SEPTIMUS
AND THE
DANEDYKE MYSTERY

faber and faber

This edition first published in 2008
by Faber and Faber Ltd
3 Queen Square, London WC1N 3AU

The right of Stephen Chance to be identified as author of this work
has been asserted in accordance with Section 77 of the
Copyright, Designs and Patents Act 1988

A CIP record for this book is available from the British Library

ISBN 978-0-571-24437-9

CONTENTS

SEPTIMUS
AND THE
DANEDYKE MYSTERY

1

The Relic Chapel

Miss Mary Crowle did not scream when she thought she saw the ghost, she continued to play the organ. She was watching her fingers as they sidled over the keys, the white ivory yellow in the soft light above the keyboard. The church around her was dark, the Jacobean pews creaking secrets to one another as they always did at night—not that Mary Crowle minded the night noises of Saint Mary's Danedyke.

She was practising Jeremiah Clarke's 'Trumpet Voluntary', which Jenny Jackson from the Home Farm had chosen for her wedding march. She did not know the piece well, so when the last child had left the village school, she had hurried through tea and housework and come along in the dusk gathering over the tumbled tombstones of the churchyard to practise. She had had some difficulty with the complicated lock the Rector had fitted to the north door. But she had managed it, frowning and tutting a little. The previous Rector had only been interested in pigs. But then he had not spent most of his life as a policeman.

She had gone to the organ—as she always did—without bothering to turn on the lights. Her practised hand had found the switch for the motor. It had sighed into life in the dark church. She had switched on the light over the keyboard and started to practise Jeremiah Clarke. She had put up her hand to turn the page of music, and her eye had gone over the top of the console into the darkness beyond, where the shadows lay.

It was then that she saw the ghost.

Beyond the empty choir stalls, on the far side of the shadowy sanctuary, where the tiny flame of the sanctuary lamp flickered was the open door to the Relic Chapel. It was there that the Danedyke Cup had once been kept, bringing pilgrims from the four corners of medieval England. It was there that Abbot John, the last abbot of the Benedictine Monastery, had been found dead. It was there that his ghost walked—so village tradition said. But Mary Crowle was fifty-five, and far too sensible to believe in village tales.

But the sanctuary lamp flickered, sending long shadows running up the walls and gleaming dully on the encaustic tiles of the sanctuary floor. And as the little flame gleamed momentarily bright, through the open doorway, standing between the chapel altar and Sir John Carruthers' tomb, Mary Crowle saw a black and shadowy figure and the gleam of a white face. And then it was gone.

Miss Crowle's fingers missed a note. She took her left hand from the keyboard, settled her spectacles more firmly on her nose, and continued to play, her heart pounding faster than she would have cared to admit. She had been a sensible, utterly devoted school teacher for thirty-five years, thirty of which she had spent in Danedyke, and she did not believe in ghosts. Anyway, she told herself firmly, no self-respecting ghost would appear while someone was playing Jeremiah Clarke's 'Trumpet Voluntary'. It was far too cheerful, even if the church was dark and what the children called 'spooky'.

She knew the legend about Abbot John well enough. She even taught it to the children in school, hoping to help them to love their parish church as she did herself. And it was a touching legend. Abbot John had been ejected when the monastery was suppressed and its treasures confiscated— including the Danedyke Cup, which was supposed to have belonged to Mary, the mother of Jesus, and to have been brought to England by Joseph of Arimathea. John had eked out a miserable existence for some ten years and had then come back to the stripped chapel which had housed the relic. There, before the ruined shrine, where the altar had once stood, he had been found dead. He was on his knees, his hands cold and rigid, clasped in prayer.

Mary Crowle stopped playing because she had run out of Jeremiah Clarke. She did *not* believe in ghosts. If there was a being in the chapel, it was alive and human. Mentally she chided her thumping heart as if it was a wayward infant.

She picked up the English Hymnal, opened it and started to play at random. The hymn was 'Rock of Ages cleft for Me'. And that was a tune suitable for a ghost. Solemn and sombre, it echoed through the empty church. Still playing, she stood up and peered across the top of the console, to the pointed shadow of the chapel door outlined by the flickering lamp. There was nothing to see but darkness. She sat down again, her fingers still playing.

> 'Could my zeal no respite know,
> Could my tears for ever flow
> All for sin could not atone:
> Thou must save, and thou alone.'

She brought the hymn to a close and sat a moment, frowning, her fingers resting lightly on the keys, the only sound the whine of the organ motor.

This was quite ridiculous. Even if Abbot John had died as the legend said, in the chapel . . . well, all human beings had to die some time, and all the village tales about cowled monks and headless horsemen were as much nonsense here in the dark church as they were in her own bright parlour in the School House. Anyway, she was a Christian.

> 'Nothing in my hand I bring
> Simply to thy cross I cling.'

She quoted the words to herself, because she had just been playing the tune. If there was anyone in the Relic Chapel it was someone belonging to the twentieth, not the sixteenth century. In fact it was probably Jimmy Bates. Jimmy was a naughty little boy, and he had an unhealthy interest in tomb-stones. In fact Jimmy had tried to remove the prayer book that the stone effigy of Sir John Carruthers was holding. He had done a great deal of expensive damage. Mary Crowle stooped down and switched off the organ motor, a frown on her face as she thought of Jimmy, and the organ motor whined into silence. She stood up smiling. Jimmy Bates was not really naughty. Only very curious. And his father was a wastrel.

She went into the vestry and switched on the choir lights, watching over the curtain as the whitewashed walls, the painted memorials and the angels of the hammer beam roof came into view. She marched across in front of the altar rails, her sensible shoes clacking on the tiles. She made a little curtsey to the altar. She stood by the door into the Relic Chapel. The interior was very black now that the choir and sanctuary were flooded with light. Her eyes behind the spectacles were screwed up because of the sudden brightness. Her heart was hardly pounding at all.

'Come out!' she said, her voice echoing down the dark nave in front of her. 'Jimmy Bates, come out this minute. You're being very naughty.'

There was silence. She paused a moment, realising soberly that she would find it very difficult to carry out the threat she was about to make. The interior of the chapel seemed so black. She took a deep breath.

'If you don't come out,' she said firmly, 'I shall come in and turn the light on.'

Nothing happened.

'Very well,' said Miss Crowle and stepped into the dark doorway.

A shape came rushing at her out of the blackness and an arm lashed across her face, hurling her aside so that she fell back-ward with a scream over the altar rail, the oak rail crashing painfully into the small of her back.

She rolled over and struggled to a sitting position, leaning against the altar itself, conscious of both the pain in her back and the curious incongruity of sitting on the altar step with her skirts round her waist. As her eyes focused she saw a dark shadow vanish beyond the reach of the choir lights down the centre aisle. She could hear running feet, and then a fumbling, and then the north door opening, and then the crash as it closed.

She was shaking as she struggled to her feet, pulling herself up by the altar frontal. Her back was very painful, and she had to retrieve her spectacles from the corner of the sanctuary. She stood with her hands on the altar and smiled weakly at the brass cross. At least it had not been a ghost. It had not been Jimmy Bates either.

The Reverend Septimus Treloar settled himself more deeply in the shabby leather armchair. Momentarily he opened a pair of blue eyes on either side of a broken nose and gazed at Miss Crowle. She was sitting very upright in the other shabby chair on the far side of the gas fire. Sir Handel, the Rector's Great Dane, was asleep at her feet, his muzzle to the fire, his big paws thrust out.

Miss Crowle's hands, which were clutching a glass of the Rector's whisky, were shaking. Both the whisky and the shaking were unusual for Mary Crowle. And she was gripping the glass as if it was a pole she was about to slide down. Mary Crowle was clearly telling the truth. Septimus smiled.

Mary Crowle thought it was a parsonical smile to encourage an elderly and rather shaken schoolmistress. Really Septimus was smiling at the cynicism and caution grained into him by thirty years in the police force. He had started as a constable pounding a beat in the East End of London just after the General Strike; he had retired as a Chief Inspector in the C.I.D. And now he was a country parson. Only a copper could have to come to the conclusion that Mary Crowle was telling the truth. For anyone else it would have been as inevitable as the dawn coming up over the North Sea.

'Tell it me all again,' he said, and closed his eyes.

'Oh but, Rector, I've already told you twice.'

'You might have forgotten something.'

He listened intently, imagining.

A man, a powerful man in the Relic Chapel. What for? There was nothing worth stealing. A Victorian cross and candlesticks which no fence would look at, which might fetch a few bob at a junk shop. It was probably no more than a down-and-out hoping to spend the night in the church.

She ended her story and gulped the rest of the whisky, making herself cough.

She said, 'I feel better now. Can I go home?'

He got up and helped her with her coat. As always she was surprised by his size and the speed and silence of his movements.

'A big cat,' she thought, 'like a great grey panther.' But what she said was, 'Thank you, Rector. I hope you don't think I'm a silly old woman.'

'No,' he said, and smiled. 'Silly old women don't give such a lucid account of an assault.'

She paused a moment before she replied, surprised by the word.

'Assault? Yes, I suppose it was. It makes it sound very dramatic. It's just as well we've got an ex-police officer as Rector.'

Despite her protests he took her home through the dark Rectory garden, down the silent village street to the School House, Sir Handel padding slowly along in the rear.

'Thank you, Rector,' she said, standing in the arched doorway.

'Mary,' he said. 'If your back's no better in the morning, you're to ring Doctor Simmonds. Rosemary can look after the school. We can't have you laid up.'

She nodded. 'Good night, Rector, and thank you.'

He strolled back along the street, deep in thought, Sir Handel pacing behind him. A down-and-out? It didn't quite fit. They did not usually strike out when they were caught.

They whined and tried to appeal to compassion. Someone who did not want to be seen . . . ?

It was closing time at the Bluebell and the clientele were turning out with a deal of shouting.

A red M.G. came out of the car park and the driver called to him.

'Good night, Squire, see you in church.' That was Tom Barton from Danedyke Garage and Rosemary Horton, Miss Crowle's pretty young assistant. They had been to see him earlier in the evening to put up their banns and had gone to the Bluebell for a celebration drink afterwards. Perhaps he would have a talk to Tom about Mary Crowle's attacker. Tom was a bright lad. He was also one of the churchwardens—the only effective one of the pair.

A bicycle passed him, weaving precariously out of the pub car park. Harry Garner, foreman at the Home Farm, the other and totally ineffective churchwarden. A churchwarden who would certainly fail a breathalyser test if they applied to bicycles. Septimus's mind skated away from the unknown man in the Relic Chapel to a consideration of the possible charges against Harry Garner. He was certainly riding dangerously, since the bicycle was going in loops from one side of the road to the other. He had no lights. It was very questionable whether the brakes on the bicycle worked. There was neither reflector at the rear, nor mudguard to carry it.

'Goo' night, Rector,' shouted Harry as they both came level with the lych-gate leading into the churchyard.

Septimus shouted a reply and watched the bicycle wander away into the night. He hoped Ted Harris, the local constable, was not waiting round the corner. It would make a tidy old village scandal if Harry Garner ended up drunk in charge.

He turned into the churchyard and walked down the path between the black yews. The church was a silhouette in front of him, spire and tower and battlements like a cutout against the deep blue sky and the stars over the North Sea.

He unlocked the north door, experiencing as always the

little glow of satisfaction at the double click of the complex deadlatch. He turned on all the lights and went to the Relic Chapel, Sir Handel following, his claws clicking on the tiles.

Nothing was disturbed in the Chapel. The two brass candlesticks and the brass cross still stood on the white cloth covering the simple stone oblong of the relic altar. The chipped stone above the altar, where once Our Lady's Cup had been enshrined, was as usual. The chairs stood as ever, awkwardly on either side of Sir John Carruthers' sixteenth-century tomb. Painted Sir John still lay, stiff as a poker, his eyes too close together, his head above a white stone ruff resting on a stone pillow. Nothing was changed. Even the single petal which had fallen from the michaelmas daisies on the window sill as he had celebrated Communion that morning, was still lying by the altar book.

Suddenly he stiffened. A policeman now, not a parson. There was a difference. Not in sight. Not in sound. The years of training and observing came to his aid. There was a difference in smell. It was very faint, but there was something that had not been there in the morning. He sniffed, wrinkling his nose like a dog at a rat hole. There was the dank smell of an unheated stone building. There was the stale smell of candle snuff. There was the smell of Brasso and of Rentokil. But there was something else. A modern smell. A mineral smell. Like Tom Barton and the Danedyke Garage. That was it! He could smell oil.

He moved suddenly, swift and silent, leaving Sir Handel standing beside Sir John Carruthers' tomb, taking out the pencil torch which he always carried. He went to the door on the outside wall, the north wall, which led out into the churchyard and over the fen. A door which once had admitted pilgrims but which was now never used because there was no point in using it. He shone the slender beam of the torch down the crack between door and post. There was a dark stain over each of the hinges and running down over the woodwork. He ran a finger over the stain and sniffed it. Oil. Someone had oiled the hinges. He put his hand to the key and turned it, moving it easily, as if the lock were in regular use. He drew the key from the lock and looked at the wards. It had been oiled as well. Then why had the intruder not escaped this way when Mary Crowle came to the door of the Chapel?

He was about to open the door, but paused with the caution of long habit, and went and turned off the light and came back across the dark chapel using the little torch. He unlocked the door and swung it open on nearly silent hinges.

The answer was obvious. Outside the door was the wire mesh of a bird grille. He shook the grille and heard the rust whispering down on to the stone step, but it did not move. It was fixed on the inside with a heavy bolt, rusted tight. The bolt had not been oiled.

He stood a moment looking through the wire over the tombstones among the tall grass at the back of the church. To the left were the trees surrounding the Rectory, and the abrupt line of the Rectory roof. To the right Danedyke Wood was silhouetted against the night. The wood was really only a spinney, and above the few trees he could see the square shape of the old lookout tower—four crumbling walls with no roof—dating from the time of Napoleon. And below it, but unseen, ran the Danedyke, straight as a ruled line from Wisbech to the Wash. And beyond the Danedyke, marsh and marram grass, mud and sandflats and the grey waters of the shallow sea.

An owl swooped low over the churchyard and fled away, calling mournfully across the fen.

Septimus closed the door and locked it. He went back to the Rectory and got Sir Handel's blanket. He laid the blanket between Sir John Carruthers' tomb and the altar rail, crumpled Sir Handel's ear and, despite the look of protest on his face, shut him in the Relic Chapel for the night.

2

The Man from Maggs

Septimus awoke instantly. Moonlight was flooding into the bedroom, and through the open window came the muffled, deep-throated barking of Sir Handel. He slid out of bed and ran barefoot across the lino. The long grass at the back of the church was blue in the moonlight, the gravestones like a scattering of white cards. He could see the outline of the Relic Chapel, but not the door. His eyes searched along the shadows by the wall of the church, but he saw no one. Then to the left, between the east end of the sanctuary and the hedge he caught a flicker of movement among the tombstones. There was a shadowy figure moving quickly, crouched down, eastward toward the boundary wall of the churchyard. It vanished into the darkness by the wall and he saw it no more. Sir Handel's barking thinned to a few scattered yells, and then the night was peaceful again.

As the church clock struck three, Septimus climbed thoughtfully back into bed and lay with his hands behind his head on the pillow. Why had the intruder gone in that direction, away from the road, toward the fen and the mudflats? There was no road, nowhere to park a car. Perhaps, after all, it was a local who would work his way along the fields at the back of the village houses and so to his own home. But what was the purpose of it all? There was little enough in the church worth stealing. The Danedyke Cup, the silver gilt relic which had supposedly belonged to Our Lady, was safe in a bank vault. The insurance company quite properly refused to entrust it to the antiquated strong box in the vestry. He smiled wryly as he thought of the strong box. He had never tried, but he fancied he could have opened it with a hairpin himself. Anyway, even if the Cup itself had been in the church, the experts said that it was not of great intrinsic value. It was supposed to be of vast antiquity, but the antiquarians said that it was really an indifferent piece of late sixteenth-century workmanship. Septimus smiled. Apparently earlier ages had had efficient operators among their forgers and conmen. Of course the Cup, because of its historical associations and the legends attached to it, might be worth a lot to an unscrupulous collector of old silver . . . There *were* such men. In his years as a policeman Septimus had seen plenty of works of art vanish without trace. His mind ran over gangs and fences . . . who was doing time, who was suspect, who was out. But his knowledge was dated and rusty, and his memory was playing tricks, and anyway, did it bear the marks of a professional job? He wasn't sure. A professional would know that the Cup was in a bank vault. Had it not been, the professional would have sized up the job for a few days. He would have been in by the north door in about two minutes (Septimus had no illusions about his fancy locks), the strong box would have taken two minutes more, and the Cup would have been in the hands of a London fence before anyone even knew it was missing. Septimus sighed. It didn't figure, and he hadn't enough material to work on. It was very fishy, none the less. He rolled on to his side and in five minutes he was asleep.

It was grey dawn with an autumnal mist rolling in from the sea when he went across to the church. Sir Handel greeted him with extravagant delight, licking his caressing hand. He opened the door leading into the churchyard. The bird grille was still in place, its rusty wire brown against the grey of the misty morning. But above the bolt which secured the grille the wire had been cut and forced inward, and the bolt had been lifted and drawn back an inch so that the rust was powdery and like cocoa on his fingertip. He considered a moment, wondering whether the bolt would yield a fingerprint. But it was too rough. He took hold of it and pulled. It squealed in protest, setting Sir Handel growling. He was about to open the grille, but paused, his eye caught by something just above the bolt. On the end of one of the severed strands of wire there was a tiny scrap of what looked like blue wool. He picked it off carefully and examined it. It looked like a piece of thread—perhaps from a tweed jacket. He put it carefully between the pages of his cheque book, opened the grille and stepped out into the churchyard, setting the mesh door groaning on unused hinges.

There was a clear track leading away from the door among the gravestones. He followed it, the wet grass soaking his trousers and ankles, to the breast-high churchyard wall. It led along the wall toward the corner with the Rectory garden where there was a short length of fence, and there he lost it. The grass in the field was too short to show tracks. He climbed into the field and Sir Handel hopped over the fence behind him. In front of him the field stretched away, its far side lost in the mist. He turned back down the outside of the wall and walked past the east end of the church until he came to the gate that led into the field. There was a barn beside it, and the gate gave on to an unmade track which led Septimus down the south wall of the churchyard and so back to the road. He looked carefully, but there were no marks of car tyres on the dirt surface, only those of a tractor. A car could have been parked on the edge of the main road under the trees, but then he had heard no sound of a car engine driving away in the night. He gave it up, went and shut the bird grille and the Chapel door, and returned to the Rectory for breakfast.

After breakfast he went across to school and took assembly. Miss Crowle was not there. Rosemary Horton had persuaded her to take the day off.

'Her back was pretty bad, Rector . . . mind out, Jimmy! You'll spill those tadpoles all over the floor. Then they'll never be frogs . . . So she stayed in bed. Doctor Simmonds is going to call in. Wait a moment, Caroline. I'm talking to the Rector. I said she ought to have told the police. But she said she had done, telling you.'

Septimus smiled. 'What has Constable Harris got, that I haven't got?'

He left her with seven-year- Caroline. It took him several minutes to get to the door of the schoolroom, as he had to stop and admire a variety of crayoned pictures, including one of himself taking a Communion service. That reminded him, and he made his way back to Rosemary.

'Rosemary, I meant to ask. Who's the local expert on the Cup?'

'The Cup,' she said, frowning. 'Why ask me? The only football I know anything about is the playground kind.'

'Our Lady's Cup.'

'Oh that!' she said. 'Doctor Simmonds, I suppose. Local history's his hobby. I think he writes articles for the County Historical Society magazine. Why do you want to know?'

'Just a thought,' he said. 'My love to Tom.' He left her coping with Mary Crowle's class and her own.

Nothing happened for three days to break the dull routine of life in the village, and Sir Handel continued to sleep in the Relic Chapel. On the fourth night the Great Dane barked again, but it was too dark to see anything from the bedroom window. In the morning the bird grille was open, the door still locked. Septimus knelt on the stone step peering into the keyhole. It was a good lock, a big hand-made affair. He doubted if it would be possible to get hold of the end of the key from the outside with a pair of pin pliers. There was a tool that would do it easily enough. A professional burglar's tool. An expensive piece of equipment which could be thrust into the keyhole and which would grip the end of the key tightly enough for it to be turned from the outside.

Late in the afternoon, on his way back in the landrover from visiting Harry Garner's wife, who was an invalid with a weak heart, he called in at the Danedyke Garage. Tom was taking the wheel off Colonel Carruthers' Rover.

'Afternoon, Squire,' he said, and held up a worn brake pad for inspection. 'Eight thousand miles since I did Pooh Bah's brakes, and look at that. Drives his car the same way he looks after the lolly. Everything at stop all the time.'

Colonel Carruthers was a descendant of Sir John Carruthers. He was an abrupt old soldier with a fierce white moustache which was why Tom called him Pooh Bah. He was also the church treasurer.

Septimus borrowed the slenderest pair of pin pliers which Tom possessed and went back to the landrover.

The light was beginning to fail when he went round to the outside of the Relic Chapel. He could get the snipe nose of the pliers into the keyhole, but could not open them wide enough to get hold of the end of the key. He was squatting back on his haunches considering the significance of this scrap of negative information when he heard the lych-gate click. There was just ten feet of the path visible between the yews, and Septimus remained still, watching the gap to see who was visiting the church so late in the afternoon.

It was a stranger carrying a parcel. He was wearing a stylish pork pie hat, slacks and a tweed jacket. The jacket was blue or it might have been green. It was difficult to tell in the failing light.

As soon as the stranger disappeared behind the yews, on impulse Septimus ran silently round the east end of the church and let himself in by the vestry door. As he closed the door softly behind him he heard the north door open. He leaned on the desk, peering through a gap in the curtains. He could hear footsteps coming swiftly up the aisle, and the stranger came into view. A small man with sandy hair and a sandy moustache, and his pork pie hat still on his head. He walked between the choir stalls and disappeared into the Relic Chapel.

Septimus went silently out of the vestry door. He ran round

the church and into the north porch, walking the last few yards, breathing deeply to still his heaving chest. He unpinned the notice about the services for the week from the board and moved until he was standing close to the door. He heard footsteps hurrying back down the aisle inside the church. He started to pin the service sheet in a new position. He heard the door start to open behind him, paused for a fraction of a second, trying to time the manoeuvre exactly, and then stepped smartly back, as if to admire the service sheet.

Septimus was large and expecting the collision, the stranger small and taken completely by surprise. He went crashing across the porch on to his hands and knees.

The Rector was profuse, abject in his apologies. He stooped, his big hands gripping the other man's coat, helping him to his feet. He brushed the stranger clumsily, gabbling apologies, a harmless teddy bear of a man in a baggy tweed suit.

'I say. My dear sir. I'm most terribly, terribly sorry. I was putting up the service sheet and I just stepped back to admire it. I'm afraid I didn't hear the door open. We've just started to use the new Mowbray's form, and I was thinking how handsome it was. I hope I didn't hurt you?'

The little ginger man was pale and trembling. It might have been because he had just been knocked across the porch. But he was no longer carrying his parcel.

'That's all right, reverend,' he said, trying to smile. 'No harm done.'

'But my dear, dear man, you're shaking. Positively shaking. You come to visit our lovely church and the Rector knocks you down in the porch. You must let me make amends. You must come and have a glass of sherry with me at the Rectory. Saint Mary's depends on its visitors, you know. You've seen our appeal for the bells? And there's the dry rot in the vestry, and death watch beetle in the hammer beam roof. You've seen our appeal? We can't have visitors saying the Rector knocks people about. You've time for a glass of sherry before you set off for London or wherever it is?'

Now the little man did manage to smile.

'Thank you, Rector. But I really haven't time. I must be on my way.'

'But I must, I simply must make amends.' Septimus waggled a finger under the stranger's nose. 'You city people! No time for our country ways. Ten minutes for Ely, five for Walsingham, and seven and a half for Saint Mary's Danedyke. Then back down the AI to Town.'

The stranger grinned nervously.

'Something like that,' he confessed. 'I called in on my way back to look at the hammer beam roof.'

'I know!' said Septimus dramatically. 'You're an architect. You work for Brewes, Jones and Wadeson. They're doing some work in York Minster. I know because I was up there last week. You've been up to York, and you're on your way back to London.'

'No,' the stranger replied. 'I've not been to York.'

Septimus looked like a bear denied a bun. 'Oh. But you *are* an architect. You must be. I suppose you've been building some terrible block of flats in Doncaster or Pontefract or somewhere?'

'Something like that.'

'I knew it. And you do work for Brewes, Jones and Wadeson? No . . . Joseph Gostaine then? No? I give up then. Those are the only architects I know. You'll have to tell me.'

'I work for a small firm called Maggs and Son. And now I really must be going.'

'Just one minute. Just thirty seconds. Wait just thirty seconds,' said Septimus and ran into the church. He grabbed a couple of picture postcards from the table and hurried out again. The stranger was already halfway down the path. He looked back hesitantly as Septimus shouted, and finally waited for him.

'My! You are in a hurry.'

'I really must get back to London, Rector.'

'Well, you will accept a little present by way of amends. A

picture of the hammer beam roof from the sanctuary or one taken from under the belfry . . . Oh no! Don't take that one, the corner's got dog-eared. There! A small amendment for knocking you down . . .'

He walked with the stranger to the end of the path and stood under the roof of the lych-gate waving as he drove away in a blue-grey Jaguar, registration number XBM 9949 C. He held the picture postcard by its folded corner, which he had himself creased in the few seconds he was in the church. He hoped its glossy surface would carry a reasonable fingerprint. He had a scrap of wool from the stranger's coat.

The Jaguar disappeared round the bend in the road and the sound of its engine faded in the dusk.

Septimus put the picture postcard gently in his pocket and tucked the thread of wool into his cheque book as he had done the piece he had found on the wire of the bird grille. Certainly it looked the same, but that was a matter for forensic experts to decide.

He went back to the church and into the Relic Chapel.

It took him about three minutes to find what the stranger had been carrying in his parcel. It lay on the floor in the narrow space between the wall and the head of Sir John Carruthers' tomb. It was a large lump of steak, and there was a white powder sprinkled liberally on top of it.

Septimus walked back to the Rectory carrying the piece of meat flat on his hand, like a waiter carrying a tray. He had to fumble with his left hand for his keys, and Sir Handel greeted him excitedly inside the front door, standing on his hind legs and sniffing avidly at the meat.

'Get down, you old fool. Gingerwhiskers only wants to poison you.'

He went to his study, shutting the dog in the corridor out-side. He laid the piece of steak on his blotting pad, ignoring the red stain which spread from its underside. He wiped his hands on his handkerchief and dropped it forgetfully on the floor. He took out the two pieces of wool and laid them on the far side of the blotter from the steak. He got three envelopes, used two of them for the scraps of wool, and using his penknife as a spoon, put some of the white powder from the steak into the third. He numbered the envelopes, then he wrote a long letter, put postcard, specimens and letter into a quarto envelope and addressed it to Chief Inspector Sam Burroughs at New Scotland Yard.

He sat for a moment considering, weighing the envelope in his hand. Then he took up the piece of steak and walked to the kitchen followed by a slavering Sir Handel. He washed the steak thoroughly under the hot tap, scalding his fingers in the process. The dog took it gently from his hand and went away into his corner.

'All contributions gratefully received,' murmured Septimus.

He posted his letter before he prepared his own supper. Then, when he had done the washing up, he went to his study and slumped in his armchair with his eyes closed. For two hours he hardly moved. Had there been anyone to see him they would have said he was asleep, but as the church clock struck ten he opened his eyes and stood up. He collected blankets from his bedroom, made sure that Sir Handel had water in his bowl, and went across to the church, moving cautiously in the blustery darkness, not using the big torch he was carrying.

He made himself as comfortable a bed as possible in the Relic Chapel, using the hard hassocks as a mattress. So he slept.

The rain was lashing the dark diamond panes of the window over the altar when he awoke. The illuminated dial of his watch was like green fire in the darkness. It was half past two. There was a scrape and a creak, a squeal of metal on metal from the door which led out into the churchyard. Silently, swiftly he threw back the blankets and followed his prepared route round the back of the chairs. He stood by the arch of the doorway, his back to the wall. Gently he stretched out a hand and put a finger—light as a moth—on the heavy key. He felt it stir and tremble and turn beneath his finger.

The door swung slowly open. The blustering of the wind

was suddenly louder. Tense behind the door, Septimus heard cautious footsteps on the tiles. He waited a moment until the intruder was fairly in the chapel, then he swung the door to with a crash, stood with his back leaning against it and switched on the big torch. Its light was of a blinding brightness, dazzling the man caught in its beam. He had spun round as Septimus slammed the door and stood for a second motionless, as if turned to stone, his hands raised as if in supplication.

It was Gingerwhiskers.

'Well, well, well,' said Septimus. 'Have you come back to have another look at the hammer beam roof?'

But even as he spoke the door handle rattled and the door was slammed violently into his back sending him staggering across the chapel, the torch spinning from his hand lighting roof and window and altar like a brief Catherine wheel before it splintered into blackness on the floor, and Septimus was falling head over heels in a welter of splintering chairs. And by the time he had extricated himself and struggled to his feet he was alone in the chapel. He staggered to the door, blundering into more chairs. He opened the door and ran full tilt into the bird grille. He leant against the rusty mesh, listening for the sound of a car engine under the sighing of the wind and the rain. But he heard nothing.

Still leaning against the grille he spoke to himself, softly but aloud. 'Septimus, you're slipping. You should have known that there would be two. Reverend Septimus Treloar, you are a bloody fool.'

3
John of Danedyke

Next day Septimus spent a dreary morning in Wisbech at a meeting about Diocesan Quotas. When it was finally over he slipped into an ironmonger's and bought a pair of heavy bolts. He drove back in the landrover along the flat straight roads through the autumn sunshine. He left the landrover outside the Rectory, collected a screwdriver and a bradawl from his workshop and went across to the Relic Chapel. He fixed the bolts to the door leading out into the churchyard and locked the internal door and took the key across to the Rectory with him.

Once back in his study, on impulse, he rang Scotland Yard and was soon speaking to the woman police constable, a big and brassy blonde, in Chief Inspector Burroughs' office.

'No, Reverend Treloar. He's gone to lunch.'

Septimus noted the 'Reverend' with a little smile.

'Joan, remind me to hear your confession next time I'm in London. Where is he?'

She giggled,

'He's gone across to the Traction Engine, sir.'

Septimus put the phone down and started again. He got the pub, and after some trouble a well-remembered voice was speaking against the background noises of the smoke room. Septimus could picture the crowded bar, blue with tobacco smoke, its walls covered with pictures of every imaginable kind of steam engine.

'Chief Inspector Burroughs speaking.'

'Sam. It's Septimus. Septimus Treloar . . .'

'Septimus! The septic reverend. And how's the one and only beatified bobby?'

'All the better for hearing your beery voice. Sam, I've got a job on . . .'

'I bet you have. Churchwarden canoodling with choir girls in the vestry . . . verger whipping the lead off the top of the organist's loo . . . sacristan forging Hymns A. and M. in the crypt . . .'

'Sam, shut up, or I'll clobber you with your own tankard next time I'm in the Traction Engine. I'm sending you some stuff for forensic . . .'

'Serious, Septimus?' The laughter went out of Sam Burroughs' voice and he was suddenly incisive, professional.

'Could be. There's a white powder someone tried to feed to Sir Handel. It's probably a barbiturate. It's not important, but I'd like to know. There's a couple of bits of wool. They don't matter now. I thought they probably came from the same villain's coat—now I know they do. The really important thing is the picture postcard with a fingerprint on it. I really want to know if Records have got a copy of that. And I want some information about art and antique jobs. You'll get my letter in the morning and—Sam—if you're not too busy, I'd be awfully glad if you could deal with it quickly. Marry you for free any time you want.'

The concern was still in Sam Burroughs' voice.

'I'll do that. But—Septimus—are you sure you don't need a copper? I mean . . . can you handle it alone?'

'Sam, when I need a copper, you'll be the last on my list.'

Chief Inspector Burroughs chuckled.

'You mad, mad clergyman.' And then more seriously, 'Take care of yourself, Septimus.'

'I'll do that, Sam.'

There was no one in the bar of the Bluebell when Septimus walked in. He ordered his usual half-pint of draught Guinness and a hot steak-and-kidney pie. He watched, leaning on the bar, while the landlord put the pie into the glass-fronted oven.

Been any strangers in, Charlie?'

'Quiet as a graveyard, Rector. The season's more or less over. Shan't see many more tourists before next year.'

'There was a foreigner in church, yesterday afternoon. Little chap. Ginger hair. Little ginger moustache and side-burns—made him look like a ponce. Blue-green Harris tweed sports coat. Pair of dark grey slacks. Brown and white—brogue style—shoes. Pointed face—sort of albino fox. Said he was an architect . . .'

'Oh him!' said the landlord. 'He wasn't in yesterday, but he was about ten days ago. Him and his mate. They were on their way up North somewhere. Driving a Jag. Right interested in the church, they were.'

'I bet they were,' said Septimus. 'What did you tell them?'

'Oh, the usual stuff. About the Cup. And the ghost stories.'

Charlie took the hot pie out of the oven and put it in front of Septimus.

'I told them about you as well,' he said. 'About you having been a detective. They seemed quite interested.'

Septimus paused with a forkful of pie halfway to his mouth.

'The devil you did,' he said slowly. 'I bet they were in-terested.'

That put quite a different complexion on matters. No won-der Gingerwhiskers had been as scared as a rabbit facing a stoat, despite the teddy bear, country parson act.

'Why, shouldn't I have?' said the landlord.

'No, that's all right. Have a drink, Charlie.'

Then as the landlord drew himself a half-pint of bitter—

'What did Gingerwhiskers' mate look like? I never met him.'

'Dunno, Rector. Big chap. Darkish. Think he had a beard. Yes, I'm sure he had a beard. Sort of nondescript. He didn't say much.'

'What was he wearing?'

'A suit? I don't really remember. It was ten. days ago. Do you want to arrest him or something?'

'No. Just interested.' Septimus gave it up. He would get no further information out of Charlie. He took his pie and tankard to a table and sat down.

So Gingerwhiskers and his mate had been in the village at least ten days ago. That pointed to professionalism, to a carefully-planned job—whatever this extraordinary job might be. And they knew they were dealing with an ex-police officer, not just any old country parson. He would have to bear that in mind. But what on earth were they up to? What conceivable reason could they have for wanting to get into the Relic Chapel in the middle of the night? He scowled a moment. It would be so much easier if they *were* trying to pinch lead from the top of the organist's loo, or to forge Hymns A. and M. in the crypt!

There was the deep-throated roar of a very large car engine from the car park outside the window. Septimus stood up and looked out. An elderly Bentley, large and red as a fire engine, was parking under the chestnut tree. It was Doctor Simmonds in Rosinante. The doctor got out of the driving seat and came toward the pub, a small man in a neat grey suit, with curly grey hair two shades lighter than the suit. He went into the snug next door, and Septimus heard his rather high-pitched voice asking for a two-ounce tin of Highland Mackenzie's Cut Plug. Doctor Simmonds had fallen out with the Danedyke Post Office, because Mrs Johnson would buy his curious tobacco in packets instead of in tins. So he had persuaded the landlord of the Bluebell to stock it for him.

Septimus picked up his tankard and his plate and went through the connecting door into the tiny snug.

'Morning, Charles,' he said. 'I've been trying to get hold of you for the last few days, but you're always out finishing off a patient.'

'Well, it keeps you in business anyway, you horrible hedge priest. Want me to beat you at chess again?' The doctor and the parson were close friends. Septimus usually won the sporadic games of chess which they played together.

'No. I wanted to talk to you about the Danedyke Cup.'

'Yes. Rosemary Horton said you did when I went to see Mary Crowle. Who's been knocking Mary about, Septimus? I don't approve. She's too valuable in this village, is Mary.'

'I take it her back's all right?'

The doctor nodded. 'She's as tough as old boots, is Mary. But it sounds—from what she told me—as if it's high time you put your uniform cap on again, Septimus. I don't suppose that turnip Ted Harris could detect a change in the weather.'

'I don't know about that,' said Septimus. 'But that was why I wanted to see you. I want you to tell me about the Cup.'

The doctor looked surprised. 'What's the Cup got to do with Mary Crowle getting knocked over the altar rail? Anyway, it would take a week to tell you about the Cup and I've got a clinic in Wisbech at three.'

'Gives you half an hour,' said Septimus, 'the way you drive Rosinante. Sit down, and I'll buy you a drink. Charlie . . . a Scotch for the doctor.' They sat on the settle by the empty grate. 'Now tell me about the Cup.'

'What do you want to know? I've got a case full of books about the Cup.'

'Not the legends. Just the facts. The real, basic, hall-marked facts, in simple language understandable by a hedge priest.'

'And you reckon they're relevant to Mary Crowle?' said the doctor, picking up his whisky and turning to look at Septimus with surprisingly keen eyes.

'Just a copper's hunch,' said Septimus, 'but it could be.'

The doctor was silent for a moment, gathering his thoughts.

'I don't approve of thugs swiping our Mary,' he said. 'I'm fond of her. Cheers, Septimus. Here's to the pregnant of Wisbech, and may the delay not be long.'

He put his glass down.

'There was a cup in the Middle Ages. Not that silver gilt fake you've got stuffed away in the bank. Saint Mary's Danedyke

Cup is mentioned in the Peterborough Chronicle—that's centuries earlier. I'd hazard a guess—a guess, mind—that the monks saw the way things were going when Henry VIII came to the throne and hid the real cup and had a replica made.'

'Could the real one still exist?' asked Septimus.

The doctor shrugged.

'It could. All things are possible—but some are not very likely. As the Apostle should have said, but didn't. Colonel Carruthers' avaricious ancestors pinched the Cup you've got when the monastery was suppressed. Saint Mary's didn't get it back until the eighteenth century. A metal cup is a fairly durable thing—unless someone melts it down to turn it into ready cash. There's a sixteenth-century poem which says,

> 'Our gay Lady's bright cup beneath Danedyke roof
> Is all faded and wan since the Beast is come.

'It amounts to this: there was a Cup long before Henry's time which everyone said was gold, and the one you've got is a piece of sixteenth-century silver gilt.'

'What other facts?' asked Septimus.

'Well, John was the last abbot. That's certain. They closed the place down and stripped the shrine in his day. Carruthers pinched the Cup—the silver gilt one—and turned the Relic Chapel into a family vault. They ejected most of the monks. Took the lead off the roof and gutted the buildings. But they seem to have left John alone for a couple of years.'

The doctor paused, sipping his drink, and thinking.

'Queer sort of life. Tragic, really. Alone in a ruined monastery. A community there five hundred years. All those abbots and you're the last, wandering about the empty cloisters and watching the rain drip through the roof. But of course they turned him out in the end.'

'What happened to him?'

'He seems to have stayed in the village. Not surprising really when you think what communications were like and remember that he wouldn't have two farthings to rub together. He seems to have run a school for farmers' sons. And he spent the rest of his time illuminating. The Benedictines were good at it and John seems to have been better than most—at least Dugdale says so. It was mostly printed books—there weren't the manuscripts, because there weren't the monasteries to write them. He did a Chaucer—that's in the British Museum. And an Ariosto—that's in the Bodleian. His Malory's gone to America—more's the pity. But the most famous was his Gospels. Dugdale called them "the abbot John's glorious Gospels". And they were manuscript by all accounts. But of course they're lost. I'd love to have seen 'em.' He paused, lighting his pipe, thinking about illuminated manuscripts.

'Do we know what happened to John in the end?' asked Septimus.

'As a matter of fact we do. There's a record of the Justice's proceedings in the Carruthers family papers. He really was found dead in the Relic Chapel. I suppose he'd gone there because the Cup had been all his life—after all, that was what the monastery was about. What's more, he'd got a will in his pocket. He left everything to the poor of Danedyke—with one exception.' The doctor paused, remembering phrases from old documents.

'Something like this . . . "I leave my few chattels to the poor of the parish, save only my copy of the Gospels of Our Blessed Lord which I have embellished over the years. These I bequeath to Simon, once abbot of the Benedictine House in Gloucester, and once my friend, if he may be found. And if not, I pray they may go to what was our house in Oxford, and is now called Abbey Hall. So may they be preserved to shine upon generations yet unborn." That was what he wrote— more or less. Abbey Hall—Gloucester College as now is.'

'And then?' Septimus asked.

'Then they vanished. Dugdale saw them in the Bodleian, so he said. But no one's seen them since the seventeenth century.'

'Thanks, Charles,' said Septimus. 'And that's the end of the hard facts? The rest is headless horsemen and hearses in the night?'

The doctor finished his drink, and looked at his watch.

'I really must go,' he said. 'But it's not quite the end of the facts. Twenty years after the Abbot John died they gave him a tombstone.'

Septimus nodded. 'I know. It's on the north wall by the door.'

'Yes. Originally it was in the churchyard—near the lych-gate. They moved it into the church sometime in the eighteenth century. It repays study, that tombstone.'

The Rector waited.

'For one thing, it's a great deal better a piece of work than you would expect. It's neatly carved, and it's literate—which is more than you can say for the usual sixteenth-century village effort.'

There was another pause, as if the doctor was expecting some reaction.

'So what do you guess, Charles?'

'I guess that an ex-monk carved it. Just a guess, mind. There's not a shred of evidence. But what did you do if you'd been a stonemason laybrother all your life, and they suddenly pitched you out into the cold world? Anyway, have a look at the carving, Septimus. It repays study. All impeccably Protestant, but you'll find some Bible texts on that stone that don't altogether figure. In fact if the Garruthers hadn't been too busy making money to look up the references, I'm quite sure they'd never have allowed it to be put up.' He looked at his watch again.

'My God, I really must go—all those pregnant mums.'

The doctor was right, the memorial to Abbot John of Dane-dyke was well executed—better than the one next to it on the north wall, and that one was two hundred years younger. It was carved in slate, the lettering a little worn by the years of exposure to the weather. Its message was short, and its Latin with the arbitrary abbreviations taxed Septimus's limited scholarship. As Charles Simmonds had said, its sentiments appeared to be impeccably Protestant. It did not even mention that John had once been that terrible thing, a Benedictine monk. It merely recorded the date of his birth and his death, and stated that he had been 'a pious man, and a learned, and ever a friend to the poor'.

In each of the four corners of the tablet there was a roundel containing one of the symbols of the four evangelists. Each improbable beast held in its paws or claws a scroll, a Bible reference written on it. The lettering was in Greek—and that was odd when the rest of the writing was in Latin, almost as if whoever had carved them did not want them to be read. Eventually Septimus managed to sort them out. Saint Luke chapter 19, verse 41. Saint Mark chapter 11, verse 17. Saint Matthew chapter 24, verse 15. Saint John chapter 11, verse 43. The Matthew reference was so indistinct that Septimus had to get up on the pew and peer closely at it with the aid of his pencil torch. Someone had scratched at the figures to make them clearer. And recently. There was a powdering of slate dust, white against the smooth grey surface of the tablet.

He went to the lectern and looked up the references in the big Bible.

'And when he was come near, he beheld the city, and wept over it.'

That was Luke's account of Jesus weeping over Jerusalem.

'And he taught, saying unto them, Is it not written, My house shall be called of all nations the house of prayer? but ye have made it a den of thieves.'

That was Mark's version of the story of Jesus throwing the money-changers out of the temple.

'When ye therefore shall see the abomination of desolation, spoken of by Daniel the prophet, stand in the holy place (whoso readeth, let him understand) . . .'

That came from Saint Matthew, and was part of the difficult chapter about the destruction of Jerusalem.

The last was the oddest of all, the quotation from John, It was a verse from the story of the raising of Lazarus from the dead.

'And when he had thus spoken, he cried with a loud voice, Lazarus, come forth.'

Septimus closed the big Bible with a thump which echoed in the silent church and stood there, unseeing, the late autumn sunshine bright on the tawdry colours of the west window.

What was it Charles Simmonds had said? Bible texts that didn't altogether figure, and the Carruthers family would never have allowed it? Three texts about destruction and desolation. Fair comment by an ex-monk on what the reformers had done to his monastery. But was that all they were— a futile gesture of contempt by a lonely and broken man? And one text about the resurrection. What was the significance of that—if it had any? Septimus gazed down the church toward the dark oblong of slate by the north door. It was as if he were listening, straining his ears for the voices of two lonely men from the remote past. But their voices were too faint, like the murmuring of ghosts rendered meaningless by the dust and decay of all the years. Then as he stood there and the sun sank across the west window, his mood changed, and it was as if the years rolled away, as if John of Danedyke might walk into the church at any moment, as if a slow chant of plainsong might come from the choir stalls behind him, as if he could hear the tap of the hammer of an unknown stonemason.

He saw through the eyes of the men who had suffered it what had happened all those years ago, the stark human tragedy behind the legends and the stiff phrases in the history books: the shrine they had loved and tended desecrated by unbelievers, their home—the great abbey to which they had devoted their lives—smashed and stripped and falling into ruin; what would seem to them the blasphemies of the Protestant rite, and the arrogant servants of Henry VIII coming in their avarice and their ignorance. Certainly they would see it as the triumph of the Prince of Darkness, as 'the abomination of desolation in the holy place'. And being men of faith, in their long loneliness they would hope against hope for a resurrection. But did they hide the Cup which had been the living heart of the whole great structure of the monastery? And if they did, had it somehow survived all the chances of the changing centuries?

Septimus sighed and ran a slow hand through his greying hair. 'A house of prayer . . . a den of thieves.' One way and another he had devoted his life to that struggle, and he also was a lonely man.

Still in the grip of the imagined past he went to the Relic Chapel, but it told him nothing. The bare slabs of the stone altar were foursquare, above them the shattered carving where once the Cup had been enshrined. Sir John Carruthers lay as he always had done, propped unnaturally on his side like a fallen statue. His painted face was calm and the blind eyes seemed to mock.

4
The Danedyke Gospels

Septimus came back from evensong, his cloak huddled around him. The autumn wind was keen from the sea now that the sun was gone.

As he walked into the Rectory the phone started to ring, setting Sir Handel barking. He went into the study and picked up the receiver without bothering to take his cloak off. It was Charles Simmonds, an excited Charles Simmonds, who started without preamble.

'Septimus? I've news for you. Someone's found the Danedyke Gospels!'

'What, since we talked at lunchtime?' There was blank disbelief in Septimus's voice. It was a policeman's reaction. He did not believe in fortunate coincidences.

'No, you ninny. Two months ago. There's an account of it in the *Bibliographical Quarterly*—I've only just got down to reading it.'

'What's that?'

'Eh? Oh. A learned journal. I only started to read it after surgery tonight . . .' The phone clicked and whirred, and then started a regular tinny hiccough. The doctor's voice went faint.

'Oh, damn this line. Look, Septimus—come up for a sherry before dinner. In fact, come now and I'll tell you all about it.'

Septimus put the phone down, called Sir Handel and they went out together into the gathering darkness. The wind was getting stronger, and the leaves were twisting down from the trees, brown in the lamplight, and swirling along the street as Septimus walked to the end of the village, beyond the street lamps, where the doctor's house stood.

Mary Simmonds answered the door and promptly invited him to dinner, but he declined, knowing that he was not expected and not wanting to disrupt her domestic arrangements. He made Sir Handel lie down in the porch and was shown into the doctor's study.

Charles Simmonds was pouring drinks at the cabinet in the corner. He greeted Septimus, thrust a glass into his hand and pointed to an open magazine lying on his desk. The magazine was a thick affair with a plain blue cover and it looked about as enticing as a police report. Septimus picked the magazine up. The article in question was headed 'Danedyke Gospels. Important discovery in Gloucester College Library.' Septimus sat down in the doctor's armchair and started to read. The first paragraph was about an American professor who rejoiced in the name of Abraham Hakenbaum and who possessed an impressive list of degrees. Apparently the American had been doing some research into what the article called 'sixteenth- and seventeenth-century black-letter editions of Reformation and post-Reformation polemical theology'. Septimus flipped over the pages. The article ran to a good twenty pages. He handed the magazine to the doctor and grinned, picking up his drink.

'It's no good, doc. The vocabulary's beyond me. I'm only an illiterate hedge priest. Just tell me what it's all about in words of one syllable.'

The doctor smiled and sat down himself, the magazine open in his hand.

'Well. There's this Yankee professor with the improbable name—Abraham Hakenbaum. He's doing some research into black-letter theological argument in the sixteenth and seventeenth centuries. It's his subject as a matter of fact—he's a world authority on it.'

Septimus was lying nearly horizontal in his chair, apparently already asleep, his glass cuddled across his cassock belt. He opened one sleepy eye.

'He's very welcome,' he murmured. And then, 'Black letter. Is that gothic stuff—like modern German, only more so?'

'Yes. Anyway, the worthy Abraham came to England on a year's sabbatical leave from his mid-western university. He goes to Gloucester College and sets about reading the Madresfield Papers from cover to cover. And he's welcome to that.'

Septimus opened both eyes. 'Why?' he asked, and closed his eyes again.

'You've never seen the Madresfield Papers. Well I have. Gloucester was my college, as a matter of fact. They're about a dozen volumes of sixteenth-and seventeenth-century texts, mostly theological pamphlets. Things like *Smectymnuus* and Milton's *Remonstrant's Defence* . . . oh! and much more obscure things. And mostly in Latin.'

'He's more than welcome,' murmured Septimus. 'I think he deserves a medal.'

The doctor consulted the magazine on his lap. 'Anyway, in the middle of volume six, Professor Hakenbaum found an illuminated manuscript, and it turns out to be the Danedyke Gospels.'

Septimus sat up slowly, putting his glass carefully on the doctor's desk.

'Charles,' he said, his eyes wide and very blue, 'I don't believe a word of it. I just don't believe it.'

'What don't you believe? That they've found the Danedyke Gospels? Well I'm telling you they have.'

'These whatsit . . . these Madresfield Papers. When were they bound?'

The doctor was suddenly pompous.

'Percival Madresfield was an eighteenth-century Irish bishop—Down and Dromore if you want to be precise. A member of Gloucester College and he left his books to the library. I suppose the collection was bound in the eighteenth century. He probably had it done himself.'

'And you mean to tell me,' said Septimus in wonder, 'that the Danedyke Gospels have been there—for two centuries—and no one's found them? I don't believe it. Doesn't anyone ever read the books in your college library?'

'My dear Septimus, have you ever tried to read black-letter theology? I don't suppose that in any generation there are more than a couple of hundred men in the world who have the equipment to read it, and of them I suppose there would be about a dozen who were in the least interested. That sort of book could easily lie unopened in a library for two hundred years until the right sort of scholarly nut-case came along. I bet there are thousands of books like that in the Bodleian.'

Septimus sighed, lay back and closed his eyes.

'I still don't believe it,' he said.

'Well you can believe it or not, but it happened. The Abbot John's Gospels have been found. But I haven't told you the really interesting bit yet. Listen to this, Septimus. You just listen . . .' The doctor started to read.

'". . . It will be realised that the study of an illuminated manuscript, even one as recent as the sixteenth century, takes time. But a cursory examination of this very late example of medieval craftsmanship yields features which are unique in my experience. While the majority of the illustrations are late examples of the usual medieval motifs, there are some which display a quite startling Renaissance modernism, as if one should suddenly discover a Book of Hours illuminated by Pieter Breughel . . ."'

'Who was he?' asked Septimus.

'Breughel? A sixteenth-century Flemish painter . . . "The photograph on page seventy-two demonstrates the point quite clearly. It shows a view of a medieval village and church, startling in its realistic detail, but in the usual tradition of medieval illumination, it is part of the ornamentation for the capital letter of the forty-first verse of the nineteenth chapter of Saint Luke's Gospel.'

Septimus shot upright, all appearance of somnolence abandoned.

'Let me see that,' he said, grabbing the journal.

The photograph showed only half of the complicated lettering of the text.

> 'And when he was come . . .
> the city, and wept over it.'

But enclosed in the capital A and surrounding it was a perfect miniature of Saint Mary's Danedyke. There were far more trees in the sixteenth century. There was no Rectory, and the whole of the abbey was still standing. And the tiny miniature was so arranged that the eye was led to its very centre where stood the Relic Chapel.

There were no other illustrations to the article.

The doctor watched Septimus with a certain amused detachment.

The priest was sitting forward in his chair, the journal forgotten on his knees, his blue eyes gazing into the distance, his mouth set in a firm line. There was a hardness about him which Charles Simmonds had never seen before, or if he had, only the merest hint of it toward the end of a hard-fought game of chess. He seemed a different man from the gentle giant to whom the doctor had grown accustomed. 'A warhorse who scents the battle from afar. Ha-ha among the trumpets.' The biblical phrases popped unbidden into the doctor's mind, but he did not voice them.

'Well, Septimus,' he said. 'Will it help over Mary Crowle's attacker?'

Slowly Septimus came back to the present. His mouth relaxed, the hoods of the eyelids dropped over the fierce blue eyes. He smiled slowly and leaned back.

'I don't know about that,' he said. 'But two things, Charles. You realise that illustration is for one of the texts on John of Danedyke's tombstone?'

'Yes,' said the doctor. 'You've been doing your homework, as I suggested.'

'Second thing, I'd like to go over to Oxford and have a look at the Gospels. How can I arrange that?'

'Already arranged,' said the doctor. 'I thought you would, so I rang the librarian after I rang you. I've cancelled tomorrow morning's surgery. We'll go in Rosinante. Tomorrow suit you? About nine thirty?'

'I'll see you in the morning,' said Septimus, standing up.

Sir Handel was waiting for him in the porch, and together they walked slowly down the village street. The wind was keen, but Septimus hardly noticed it, his thoughts were in too much of a torrent. If the Danedyke Gospels carried one 'modern' illustration of one of the texts from John of Danedyke's memorial stone, what about the other three? If Danedyke village and church was 'the city over which Jesus wept', what was the 'den of thieves' and what was the 'abomination of desolation'? And was there a real connection between the references on the stone and the Gospels—or was it pure chance? And did it have anything to do with Our Lady's Cup? And did it have anything to do with Mary Crowle's attacker and the curious attempts to get into the Relic Chapel? And if all these things were connected—what in heaven's name had Lazarus to do with it? He shrugged his shoulders and started to whistle a hymn tune. He still hadn't enough facts to go on, so speculation was useless. He quickened his pace back to the Rectory.

He spent the night in the Relic Chapel, taking Sir Handel with him this time. Not that he expected a further attempt to break in after the events of the previous night. Surely Gingerwhiskers and his accomplice would have been scared off for at least a few days. Perhaps they would have been scared off for good— but Septimus doubted it. Even so, he was concerned to keep all safe until he had been to Oxford. Perhaps the Danedyke Gospels would provide the key to what was going on.

He settled down on the hard mattress of hassocks, Sir Handel on a blanket beside him, the wind rattling the windows, and the timbers of the church creaking and cracking beyond the open door.

Sir Handel started to bark at nearly three o'clock and Septimus snapped awake immediately. He could hear nothing from the firmly-bolted door; there were only the night noises of the church as the wind whistled around the walls. Even so he ran across the choir and out through the vestry door, and round the east end. There was no sign of anyone in the church-yard, only a fitful moon playing hide-and-seek behind stormy clouds and the wind whispering through the long grass and moaning over the unseen battlements of the church, and Sir Handel barking enthusiastically on the other side of the Relic Chapel door.

'Quiet, you fool,' shouted Septimus at the keyhole, and the big dog lapsed into aggrieved silence. Then there was nothing but the night wind. Slowly he walked round the building and back into the church. He made Sir Handel lie down and sat for a while on the chapel altar rail, close to the door leading into the choir, his ears analysing the noises of the night. The wind was muted, but the old building muttered its own secrets: the cracking of timber, the rattle of a loose pane of glass, the creak of a bell rope swinging in the draught under the tower, the rustle of a mouse behind the oak panelling of the sanctuary. There was nothing else. And in sight there was only the rise and fall of the sanctuary lamp through the arched doorway and the shadows of the trees tossing across the windows.

Satisfied at last, but still no wiser, he went to his hard bed of hassocks. Sir Handel was already fast asleep and whimpering as he hunted in his dreams.

5

To Oxford . . .

If the near side wing mirror of Rosinante, Doctor Simmonds' immaculate red Bentley, had not been wrongly adjusted, Septimus might not have noticed that they were being followed. Charles had insisted on using Rosinante, as the Rector had feared he would. He loved the car very dearly and drove it far too fast, so Septimus composed himself as best he could for sleep in the passenger seat as they set off with a jerk for Oxford. He did not open his eyes until they paused under the gracious eighteenth-century frontages of Wisbech, waiting to cross the river Nene. From sheer force of driving habit he glanced up to his left as if he were at the wheel, realised in that split second that he was in the passenger seat, and so let his eyes drop to the wing mirror on the near side of the Bentley. The mirror was twisted so that he could see the bonnet and windscreen of the car behind. It was a blue-grey Jaguar. The driver was big, with a short beard and dark hair which sat close to his head like a cap of ebony. Septimus wondered whether the number was XBM 9949 C, but thought it not very likely. It was almost certainly a coincidence. Blue-grey Jaguars were not all that uncommon. But the Jaguar was still behind them as they drove into Peterborough.

At they stopped at the lights by the entrance to the Cathedral Septimus stretched up his hand to the interior mirror.

'Charles, d'you mind if I borrow your mirror for a few miles? You can drive just as dangerously on your wing mirror.'

The doctor grinned and took the Bentley snarling round a cattle truck at the last available moment before a double white line.

'Playing cops and robbers with the Jag, Septimus? He's been trying to pass Rosinante since Wisbech.'

'That's what I want to know about,' said Septimus, adjusting the mirror. The Jaguar came into his view round the curve behind them, but it was too far back to read the number plate. It was three cars behind them as they crossed the AI at Kate's Cabin, and remained three cars behind them all the way to Oundle despite the fact that Charles, prodded by Septimus, dropped the speed of the big Bentley to a mere forty miles an hour. Beyond Oundle, once again prodded by Septimus, the doctor nursed Rosinante up to an illegal and highly dangerous ninety. This had the effect of separating the men from the boys, and as they drew into Northampton, braking sharply to a legal thirty, the Jaguar was suddenly close behind them. By fiddling with the mirror and by half standing up, Septimus managed to get a look at the number plate without actually turning round—which was the last thing he wanted to do.

XBM 99 . . . something or other. But that was good enough. It was the car that Gingerwhiskers had driven away in after Septimus had knocked him down in the church porch. And it was the number two villain driving it. A big man with a beard who seemed somehow vaguely familiar. But the important thing was that Gingerwhiskers was not in the passenger seat—which meant that he could be in Dane-dyke planning all sorts of mischief. Septimus began to feel uncomfortable about the Relic Chapel. Daylight would be no sort of protection for it if Gingerwhiskers knew that he was halfway to Oxford.

The road rose suddenly on to a bridge and Septimus found himself looking down at twin streams of traffic speeding north and south. They were crossing the MI. He looked up at the mirror. The Jaguar was not in sight. He sat up, frowning, adjusting the mirror to hold the point where the road curved out of sight behind them.

'Slow down, doc,' he said, gazing hungrily at the mirror.

They trundled into Towcester at a sedate thirty, but the Jaguar did not reappear.

Furiously, Septimus set himself to think of the reasons. So remote that it was almost over the horizon was the possibility that he had misread the number plate and the Jaguar belonged to a shoe manufacturer who kept a mistress in Wisbech and was going back to his factory after a dirty night and a late breakfast. Or something like that. The more realistic possibilities were not pleasant. Granted the Jaguar belonged to the opposition, either it had turned back, satisfied that they were on the way to Oxford, or the driver had stopped to make a phone call—presumably to Gingerwhiskers. Either way the significance was the same. Septimus, the Rector, the ex-policeman, the owner of that damned dog, was comfortably out of the way, and the Relic Chapel was wide open to any sort of assault.

There was a pub called the Red Cow on the left.

'Pull into the pub car park!' said Septimus suddenly, and as Rosinante screamed to a halt across the tarmac he shot out of the door leaving the doctor to keep watch and ward for the Jaguar.

The bar was nearly empty, and the barmaid looked at Septimus in some surprise, perhaps because of his haste, more likely because of his clerical collar.

'A phone,' he said. 'It's most important.'

She looked doubtful. 'Well, Reverend, there is one, but the guv'nor doesn't like customers using it. It's private.'

'Please,' he said. 'It really is urgent.'

She went through the curtain behind the bar and came back with the landlord, a fat little man, rather self-important, who was not keen to allow Septimus to use the phone. There was a public call box on the corner,

Septimus took a pound out of his wallet and laid it on the

46

bar. He leaned across, his face six inches from the publican's.

'I must use that phone,' he whispered conspiratorially. 'Don't be misled by my clerical collar. MI5. I could show you my identification and explain—but there's no time.' He winked solemnly in the face of the astonished publican, whose eyes went round as pennies as he opened the flap of the bar.

'Thank you,' said Septimus solemnly. 'We won't forget.'

There was no dialling code for Danedyke Saint Mary so Septimus had to wait for the operator. Her voice was metallic and uninterested.

'I am a police officer,' said Septimus authoritatively. 'Chief Inspector Treloar speaking. This is an emergency. I've two calls to make, so keep the line if you can, there's a good girl.'

The metallic voice was now full of concern.

Septimus gave the number and waited. The publican's face came round the door. Septimus winked at him, listening to the ringing tone.

Mary Crowle answered the phone.

'Mary? The Rector here . . . yes, the Rector. Look. I want you to do something for me. It's to do with the man who attacked you. I don't want the church unattended this afternoon. Could you spend all afternoon doing history with the school? Take them into the churchyard. Study tombstones and things. Fonts and carvings. Especially the Relic Chapel. Keep the place full of children until four o'clock.' He paused, listening to her surprise, helping her get used to the odd request. Good old Mary. She caught on incredibly quickly.

'No,' he said. 'There's no danger. None at all. Safety in numbers. Kids crawling all over the pews. Bless you. Good-bye.'

He clicked the phone and the operator replied immediately, her voice sharp with suspicion.

'You said you were a police officer. You sound like a parson.'

'Yes,' he said easily, 'but the clerical collar's a disguise. Now get me Danedyke Saint Mary 239.'

Tom Barton answered from the Danedyke Garage.

'Tom? It's the Rector here. Look. I'm in a deuce of a hurry. You remember what I told you about Mary Crowle and the Cup? . . . Yes. That's right. Well I'm on my way to Oxford and I don't want the church left unguarded until I get back . . . No, I can't explain now. I've arranged for the school to be there all afternoon, but they'll go home at four. Now look, Tom, will you please close the garage at four and go and cut the grass outside the Relic Chapel until I get back? What? . . . I don't give a hang about that. Rosemary can come and help you . . . Yes. It matters. It really matters. Bless you. I'll explain later.'

He put the receiver down and ran out of the bar shouting his thanks as he went.

Charles Simmonds started Rosinante as Septimus came out of the door.

'The Jaguar went past three minutes ago,' he said, 'driving like the clappers.'

'Did he see you?'

'I imagine so. Rosinante isn't exactly self-effacing.'

Septimus cursed himself as they pulled away from the Red Cow. They should have concealed the car.

'Oh well, we'll soon know,' he said. 'He'll pull off the road and wait for us to pass.' Still, it had been worth stopping. He felt easier in his mind about the Chapel. He grinned to himself, thinking of Gingerwhiskers concealed in the hedge mournfully surveying a churchyard full of small children.

'Our friend has reappeared,' said the doctor.

Septimus glanced up at the mirror. The Jaguar was fifty yards behind.

'Okay, Charles,' he said. 'He obviously knows we're going to Oxford, but you can give him a run for his money.'

The doctor smiled sideways.

'Can I have my driving mirror back?' He adjusted it, dropped into third, and sent Rosinante snarling round a furniture van into an apparently impossible gap before the beginning of a double white line and an oncoming stream of traffic.

Septimus closed his eyes.

'My God,' he said. 'That I should live to give permission for such flouting of the Road Traffic Act.'

They were running into Oxford as the clocks struck noon, and they had seen nothing of the Jaguar for twenty minutes.

They left the Bentley outside the mock gothic front of Gloucester College in a space marked 'Reserved for the Dean'. Septimus made no comment. It was, after all, Charles Simmonds' old college.

The doctor led the way through the little door in the massive oak ones which filled the pointed arch. The porter, a large man with a little pointed moustache surveyed them with disfavour from his glass box.

'Afternoon, Giles,' said the doctor, waving an airy hand.

'Sir!' Doctor Simmonds, sir. You know you can't leave your car there, sir. That's the Dean's space, that is.'

'It *is* Montgomery, Giles. The Dean's painted it red.' Then they were round the corner, leaving an aggrieved Giles calling after them. The doctor led the way along a cloister beside an immaculate lawn and up a circular staircase, explaining as he went.

'The Dean,' he said. 'Colonel John Bulstrode. He runs a Bentley identical to Rosinante—only two years younger and painted blue. He calls it Montgomery. We were up together. Had rooms on the same staircase. He ran an old Alvis in those days, and I had a bull-nosed Morris. I raced him to Land's End and back. He won. The blighter put sugar in my petrol tank. Stranded me in Redruth. I was M.O. to his regiment in the war. We were at Alamein together.'

The library was a vast, eighteenth-century room with a gallery running round its walls and seven gracious, round-headed windows. Mr Empson the librarian was expecting them. He greeted them eagerly, excitedly. The discovery of the Danedyke Gospels was far and away the most important thing that had ever happened in his placid life. Volume 6 of the Madresfield Papers was laid on an oak table, ready for them.

It was a fat quarto, bound in blue morocco, with an elegant gold tooled eighteenth-century design on the leather.

The librarian opened the book, ruffling through the pages to find what he wanted. Septimus could see the uninviting black-letter printing on the foxed paper. It was easier to understand, when one actually saw those black slabs of print, how a book could remain unread for two hundred years.

'There!' said Mr Empson triumphantly, holding the quarto open with loving hands.

All was different. The shabby paper, the smudged printing were gone. In their place was pure vellum, tinted like old ivory, delicate lettering, fresh as spring flowers, the colours leaping from the page as if they had just been painted.

'The Gospel According to Saint Matthew.' Septimus read the complex lettering on the title page. But it was not just a page in a book. It was like. . . what was it like? It was like looking at a medieval garden. It was like what he had felt when police business had taken him to Chartres, and he had spent a hot summer afternoon wandering in the cool of the cathedral.

'It's like Chaucer's *Book of the Duchess* come to life,' said the doctor in awe.

Forgetful of the librarian, they slowly turned the pages, lost for a moment in the beauty of John of Danedyke's masterpiece.

It was Septimus who brought them back to reality. He pulled a notebook from his pocket and looked up the references.

'Matthew twenty-four, fifteen,' he said. 'The abomination of desolation.'

The doctor turned the stiff pages with careful hands.

Matthew twenty-three, twelve . . . and then Matthew twenty-four, twenty-five. The page was missing. They turned back to make sure, and the doctor peered down into the binding.

'It's not been cut out,' he said. 'It's never been bound in this volume.' The librarian spoke from behind them.

'Professor Hakenbaum's research assistant noticed that that leaf was missing. He was most interested in the fact.'

Septimus looked down at the librarian, a thin-faced nervous young man, innocent of all guile. There was a seed of doubt in Septimus's mind. Did American professors on overseas tours go in for research assistants? He left the matter for the moment and turned back to the book.

'Mark eleven, seventeen,' he said. 'That's the one about the house of prayer becoming a den of thieves.'

That page was not missing. Its ornamentation was most elaborate, and at first they could see nothing unusual about it.

It's beautiful, 'said the doctor.' But so what? So's all the rest.'

'It was Professor Hakenbaum who first saw it,' said the librarian. 'Look at the capital A through this.' He gave a powerful magnifying glass to the doctor, who bent close over the book.

'Good Lord,' he said softly. 'It's the Relic Chapel.'

Septimus took the glass. A moment to adjust the powerful lens, and then he found himself gazing at a perfect miniature of the interior of the chapel. The chapel not as it was in the twentieth century, but as it must have been in the sixteenth, before the troubles of the Reformation. The view was from the back—where Sir John Carruthers' tomb now stood. In the centre of the picture was the altar, the window above it full of stained glass, and between altar and window where now was only broken stone, there was an ornamented shrine. All the lines of the picture led to a bright dot of gold in the centre of the shrine. Presumably it was Our Lady's Cup.

They did not spend long on the illustration of the text from Saint Luke, since that was the one reproduced in the *Bibliographical Quarterly*, but turned on to Saint John, to the quotation from the story of Lazarus. Here a further surprise awaited them. The illustrator had abandoned almost all the medieval conventions. Down the whole of the inside of the vellum page was a picture of a man. A man painted in greens and blues, a repulsive man wrapped in leprous bandages, shuffling out of the page with one shoulder forward. It was clearly an unwilling

Lazarus, a Lazarus with all the indignity and decay of death still about him, shuffling back to the bright day. But his bandaged hands were clutching to his chest a bright golden cup. In the proportion of the painting it must have been two feet high, and its gold glowed so that it dominated the page, and it was the same shape as the cup in the bank vault.

There was nothing more they wanted to see, so the doctor led the way down to the buttery for a sandwich and a beer.

The buttery proved to be one of those college bars which only Oxford can provide. A low-beamed room, much in need of redecorating, and of great age. Its walls were covered with trophies: pictures, postcards, medals, flags, photographs from the last half-century and from the ends of the world. Trophies of the Everest expedition rubbed shoulders with a picture of a fat woman on Brighton beach. There was a nineteenth-century policeman's helmet next to an M.C. in a glass case. Septimus left the doctor and the librarian and took his tankard and crab sandwich outside and sat beneath a cedar tree in the autumn sunshine. He wanted to think.

Three pictures—and one missing, Matthew unaccounted for. Mark—that was a picture of the inside of the chapel. Luke—that was a general view of the monastery with the chapel at its centre. And John—that was Lazarus holding the Cup. The Lazarus story was about a resurrection. Perhaps the restoration of the Cup was the resurrection that Joan of Danedyke had had in mind when he painted the picture.

Suppose . . . suppose John had hidden the real Cup and had the silver gilt replica made to take its place, hoping that there would be a reversal in the tide of religious opinion. Suppose that as those who knew the secret died, John had used his Gospels as a means of saying where the Cup was hidden. He had, after all, left the Gospels to another ex-Benedictine monk, and if the monastery had been restored eventually someone in sympathy with the old ways might have guessed the secret. Certainly it would keep the secret from the Protestants, who were not interested in illuminated manuscripts.

But if the pictures were clues to the hiding place, they did not say anything. Their order was meaningless.

> 'Matthew, Mark, Luke and John
> Bless the bed that I lie on.'

Septimus quoted the old prayer to himself. But did they have to be in that order? The roundels on John's tombstone were not. And that was an odd thought! He closed his eyes, trying to remember. Top left—Luke. Top right—Mark. Bottom left—Matthew. Bottom right—John.

> 'Luke, Mark, Matthew, John
> Bless the job that I am on.'

In terms of the pictures, that gave first a general view of the monastery with the Relic Chapel in the middle of it; then a view of the interior of the chapel; then a blank; then the picture of Lazarus coming back from the dead, carrying the Cup. Septimus suddenly remembered the scratch marks on the Saint Matthew reference on John of Danedyke's stone and everything slid into place, and he jumped to his feet, convinced that he now knew as much about the Cup as the opposition did.

Of course! First the church itself, then the chapel, then the missing picture would have showed where to look in the chapel, and the fourth one showed what you would find there. And John of Danedyke had died, and an unknown stonemason had carved the texts on his memorial in order that the secret might not be lost altogether.

But Gingerwhiskers and his accomplice did not know where to look in the Relic Chapel. So, they wanted to get into it secretly at night, because they wanted to take the Chapel apart in their quest for the Cup. And at the back of them was probably somebody knowledgeable in old gold and silver who thought that there was a pretty fair chance that the original Cup was still in existence.

6

. . . And Back

The librarian and the doctor were sitting companionably on a black oak settle before the stone cavern of the buttery fireplace. The librarian was a voluble young man, eager to answer Septimus's questions.

Yes, Professor Hakenbaum had come to the college much earlier in the year. In April, toward the end of the Hilary Term. No, his research assistant had not come with him. He had been sent by the professor only a few weeks ago to check one or two things in the Gospels. He had a letter of introduction from the Professor. Well, the letter was *signed* by the Professor, so presumably it was *written* by the Professor.

The research assistant was called Mr Jones. He was doing graduate research at London University. Yes, Mr Jones was a small man with sandy hair and a sandy moustache. Did the Rector know him? Septimus did not answer the librarian's question. He was digesting the information he had gleaned.

'Did Mr Jones leave you any instructions?' he asked.

'Oh, yes. Like you, Rector, he was most interested in the missing page. He said the Professor would like to know if by any chance it turned up. I must say it seems hardly likely. But I promised to let him know if it did.'

'He left a forwarding address, then?' Momentarily Septimus's sleepy blue eyes betrayed surprise.

'A box number in Wisbech. It seemed rather surprising for a graduate of London University, but Mr Jones explained that he was doing some research in East Anglia.'

Septimus took out a visiting card and handed it to the librarian.

'Mr Empson, if that missing page did by any chance turn up, I would be most grateful if you would ring me first of all. After all, it concerns my church, and I should be glad to be forewarned before Mr Jones or any other scholar descended on me. One feels such a fool if one doesn't know what people are talking about.'

'Yes, of course, Rector. You shall know before anyone else. As you say—it *is* your church.'

They said their farewells and went away down the cloister.

The porter was waiting for them, towering by his little glass box, like a beefeater in mufti.

'Doctor Simmonds, sir,' he barked with immense disapproval in his voice. 'That there's not the Dean's car. The number's different.'

The doctor smiled up at him as they marched past. 'That's right, Giles,' he said. 'He changes the number with the paint— like women's hats . . .' They had passed through the door before Giles had sorted out this ambiguous sentence.

In the Dean's parking space Rosinante gleamed like a fire engine in the autumn sunshine. But Rosinante's bonnet was up, and a man was stooping over the engine.

'Hey!' shouted the doctor as he ran. 'Stop that!'

Septimus paused for a fraction of a second, taking in the scene: the bearded villain looking up, startled; the Jaguar parked illegally at the kerb, its door open; the woman with a pram coming along the pavement and frowning as she had to negotiate the open door of the car. Then Septimus ran—not toward Rosinante, but toward the Jaguar.

Had it not been for the pram Septimus would have won the race. As it was the bearded man shot round the back of the woman and dived into the driving seat, leaving the door to slam itself shut as he screeched away from the kerb, and Septimus found himself lying across the pram, a squawling infant beneath his midriff, an angry matron towering above him. He hauled himself off the pram and turned to face the woman. Mostly she seemed to be cross that he was a clergyman, so at last he quelled her by saying, 'Yes, madam. I am a clergyman. I am Dean of this college. I am humbly sorry that I overlaid your infant. But that man was stealing my motor car.'

She gathered breath and renewed the assault.

'Well, if you're a Dean and not a common clergyman that only makes it worse. And if that man has stolen your motor car, I hope he drives it into a lamp post before you can find a policeman.'

She sniffed at him and marched away, her head in the air, her bottom waggling, her offspring still wailing.

Septimus watched her go, his big hands hanging helplessly by his side. There was a surrealist quality about the espisode which made him want to laugh. He could indeed find a policeman. 'Ah, officer,' he would say, 'there's a man driving a blue-grey Jaguar, registration number XBM 9949 C. He's just interfered with Rosinante.'

'Yes, sir. And who's Rosinante? A choir boy, sir?'

Septimus's shoulders started to shake and he walked back toward the Bentley. The doctor was standing, arm outstretched, one finger pointing at the disclosed works of his motor car. It reminded Septimus of a tomb in Saint Mary's churchyard where a marble Angel of Death stretched out a white arm and accusing finger at a marble skull.

'He's pinched Rosinante's rotor arm!' The doctor's face was red, his voice squeaky with anger.

Septimus sat on the running board and buried his face in his hands. He could feel the tears of laughter running between his fingers.

'Officer,' he would say to the constable with his serviceable bicycle and rusty cycle clips round his uniformed ankles, 'Officer, he pinched Rosinante's rotor arm.'

And the constable would lick his pencil, and frown and push back his helmet. 'And what part of the anatomy is that, sir?'

'I don't know what the hell you're laughing about, you

stupid no-parson, 'snapped the doctor.' What are we going to do about Rosinante's rotor arm? Are you going to run round and round in little circles with sparks flying out of your ears?'

Septimus wiped his eyes and blew his nose. It really was rather serious. They had to get back to Danedyke Saint Mary.

'Bentley agent?' he suggested.

'Not a hope,' snapped the doctor.

'Well, we'll have to hire a car, then,' said Septimus. 'We've got to get back—and quick. Tom won't go on cutting that grass all night.'

But the doctor was not listening. There was a faraway look in his eyes, and he had forgotten to be angry.

'There's always Montgomery,' he said. 'Her distributor's the same as Rosinante's. Now if Johnnie Bulstrode has gone off to some don's wife's bunfight and left Montgomery in the garage . . . Come on, Septimus. Let's indulge in some borrowing or a little bit of larceny.' He led the way along the college wall to the Dean's house.

Despite his sense of urgency, Septimus was still inclined to burst into laughter.

'Are you proposing to pinch the Dean's distributor?' he asked.

'Not me. You,' said the doctor. 'You were a copper. Ought to be able to manage a little matter like forcing a yale lock.' The doctor grinned suddenly. 'I'll teach Johnnie to put sugar in my petrol tank. Strand me in Redruth, would he?'

They pealed on the bell beside the imposing front door, but there was no reply. They went round the side of the house, the gravel crunching beneath their feet. The green garage doors were locked, but the side windows revealed that Montgomery was in residence.

The doctor rattled the doors.

'Show us what you can do, Septimus,' he said.

Septimus smiled. 'It's your prints on the door handle,' he replied.

He took out his pocket knife and a plastic bank card. Thirty seconds later the doors were open. The doctor was most impressed.

'Are you sure you were a Chief Inspector, and not a cracksman?' he asked.

'Just professional expertise,' Septimus replied as they opened the bonnet of the blue Bentley. While Septimus extracted the rotor arm, the doctor took a prescription pad from his pocket and wrote a note.

Dear Johnny,
    I've borrowed Montgomery's rotor arm, a rogue having pinched Rosinante's, and I've got to get back for surgery. I'll post it to you tomorrow. If you tell the police I shall sell the true story of the Land's End race to *The News of the World*.
Yours,
Charles.
PS.—The chief inspector who burgled your garage for me doesn't think much of your locks.

They left Montgomery's bonnet open and impaled the note on the spike of one of the bonnet strap buckles.

It was nearly five o'clock when Charles Simmonds turned Rosinante into the Rectory drive. Septimus climbed stiffly down, thanked the doctor and watched while he turned the car and drove away.

He could hear the high-pitched whine of the rotor scythe from the churchyard on the far side of the hedge. Tom Barton could wait five minutes more while he had a word with Sir Handel. He walked into the Rectory, whistling for the dog, but there was no welcoming bark. He went into the gloomy kitchen. Sir Handel was not there, but there was a chair knocked on its side, and Sir Handel's water was spilled in a wide puddle about his bowl, and there were dog biscuits scattered across the floor. With a sense of foreboding he turned on the light, and started to make a serious examination of the room.

Someone had forced the window over the sink. The catch was back, and he could see the scratches of the tool which had been used. The kitchen door was unlocked, the key still on the inside, and there was a dark smear on the stone flags between the coconut matting and the door. He ran a finger across it, but it was dry. He licked the finger and tried again, and this time the tip of his finger was dark brown. It was probably blood. There was a tuft of brindled hair caught in the angle of the metal surround of the doormat well.

He opened the back door and went out. The sun was low in the west, the shadows long across the uncut grass. The gravel was scuffed, and it was easy to see where the grass had been trampled down in a track leading to the spinney.

He found Sir Handel ten feet inside the spinney. The dog was lying in a hollow under a bramble bush, and he was dead, a great blood-encrusted wound across one crumpled ear. His lips were drawn back in a snarl, and between his white teeth was clenched a piece of tweed. Septimus did not need to take it from the locked jaws. He knew the coat it had come from.

He stood up in the twilight of the copse, his face like stone. The laughter of the earlier part of the day seemed to belong to another century. Dry-eyed, he faced facts. In all his years with the police he had investigated murders, rapes, bank robberies, kidnappings. He had sent men to prison for more years than he cared to contemplate. He had sent four men to the gallows. In that time he had often been threatened with violence. But it had not meant much, because you could keep your job and your personal life separate. But now he was no longer a police officer he could not separate the one from the other. He was personally involved. And Sir Handel was dead.

He crouched down and pulled two strands of the tweed from between the dog's locked jaws. Obscurely he felt it would be the final indignity to prise those great teeth apart, to take away for all time what little Sir Handel had won in the face of death. But professionalism demanded its tribute, and evidence was evidence.

He put the strands of wool into his wallet and then, aware of the curiousness of the action, he gently closed the staring eyes. He picked up the great body, stiff and ridiculous in death, and carried it cradled in his arms back to the Rectory.

7
Night Attack

The phone was ringing. Septimus laid Sir Handel's body on the kitchen floor and went through to the study.

'Septimus? It's Sam. Sam Burroughs. I got your letter. It'll take a bit of time to compile the Interpol list—but I've put it in hand. The white powder was a barbiturate. Basis of half a dozen proprietary sleeping pills. Do you want to know which one?'

'No. It doesn't matter now.'

'And the pieces of wool. They are from the same material. Cheapish cloth. Probably an imitation Harris Tweed. Bluish in colour—though of course it might have been a check.'

There was a silence. Septimus was thinking of the piece of cloth clamped between Sir Handel's teeth.

'Septimus, are you all right?'

He wanted to say 'The bastards have killed Sir Handel', but he did not. The wound was too raw, the phone too impersonal.

'Yes, I'm all right, Sam. Just thinking. What about the print on the postcard?'

'Nothing in records, I'm afraid. If he's a villain we've never caught him.'

'Well, I'm very grateful, Sam, and I shall be glad to get that list.' Bye for now. Tell you all about it over a jar sometime.'

Tom Barton switched off the rotor scythe as Septimus came through the gate from the Rectory. Rosemary Horton jumped off the tombstone on which she was sitting and they came together to greet him, Tom's arm round Rosemary's waist.

'Fine old jet-propelled mangle that rotor scythe is,' said Tom. 'Can't think what you do with it after I've serviced it. Prune the barbed wire?'

Septimus told them about Sir Handel.

'Oh, how horrible,' said Rosemary. 'But why, Septimus? Why would anyone want to kill Sir Handel?' He looked at her for a long moment. Her fair hair was almost auburn in the dying sun. She was very pretty and very young. She made him feel old and tainted by all the evil he had seen, by all the greed and wanton destruction.

'Because he was in the way,' he said heavily. 'Because I put him in the Chapel and he saw them off a couple of times.'

Tom smoothed back a lock of his lank hair, leaving a streak of grease on his forehead.

'Does that mean they're going to have another go?' he asked.

'Yes,' said Septimus. 'And this time I'm going to nail them, not just stop them.' He told them the events of the day.

'So they think the Cup's still in the Chapel,' he ended. 'And, by God, they mean to get it. Poor old Sir Handel. I hope he took a chunk out of that villain's arm as well as out of his coat.'

Rosemary stamped on the path.

'But why?' she said angrily. 'Why? An old gold cup. What's it worth? You'd never be able to sell it.'

Septimus smiled at her. He felt like Grabbed Age facing Youth.

'What would you give for it, Rosemary?'

She frowned. 'I don't know. Fifty pounds. A hundred pounds if I wanted it very much.'

'If you'd got a hundred pounds,' said Tom.

'Beast!' she said.

'But there are people who would pay ten thousand for it,' said Septimus. 'Not many. But they do exist.'

Her face was screwed up in puzzlement. 'But what for? What on earth for?'

He shrugged. 'So you can look at it and think, I've got it and no one else has. Just me and it. I'm unique.'

'It doesn't make sense,' she said.

'No. But it happens. I once nobbled a character who thieved a vase from the London and Middlesex Museum. A thing that looked like a Victorian lustreware po without a handle. He got six months and we didn't catch anyone else. But a London fence had given him five hundred pounds for it. I traced it back through three other people—no proof, of course. But by then the price had risen to five thousand. Apparently it was some unique Chinese piece, and somewhere there was a rich character who just wanted to gloat over it in secrecy and silence.'

'My baby,' said Rosemary, scuffing the gravel with her foot. 'Mine and no one else's. But I didn't bear it, I bought it.' She shuddered. 'It makes my blood run cold.'

Tom helped Septimus to dig a grave for Sir Handel under an apple tree in the overgrown orchard at the back of the Rectory, talking cheerfully as they burrowed into the black earth, making conversation because of the macabre nature of the task. It did help, and in grateful response Septimus told Tom the plan he had worked out on the drive back from Oxford.

At last the black hole was deep enough, and as if by agreement they went to the kitchen, silent now, and came back with

Sir Handel and laid him in the earth. Silently they filled the hole in, silently they went back to the Rectory.

Rosemary had tidied the kitchen and washed the smear of dried blood from the floor. Sir Handel's bowls had vanished from their place by the old range and his blanket had been put away. The kitchen looked empty. Rosemary was right of course, but it hurt all the same.

She put a slender arm round his shoulder, and standing on tiptoe kissed him on the cheek. 'I've tidied up the kitchen,' she said.

'Hey, come off it!' said Tom. 'He wants a hundred and fifty yards of cable from the garage before he goes to bed. You can kiss me when we've delivered that.' They went off in Tom's car, leaving Septimus to gather the other bits of equipment that he needed for the execution of his plan. The time for guarding the Relic Chapel was past. Now he was going to catch the intruders.

He went across to the church and with some difficulty extracted the ladder from its resting place under the tower. He carried it round the church and reared it against the gable end of the Chapel; then he went back to the Rectory. Tom and Rosemary arrived, carrying a big reel of five-amp cable between them. They took the cable up to Septimus's bedroom, tied the loose end of the cable to the leg of the bed and dropped the reel out of the window with a thump on to the lawn. They went down and picked up the reel and paid the cable out, across the lawn and garden, over the hedge, and across the churchyard to the Chapel.

It was very quiet in the churchyard. The autumn wind had dropped with the coming of night. Most of the birds were silent, and only a few rooks called from the elms by the Manor where Colonel Carruthers lived. The light was fading fast, but it would serve.

Tom went up the ladder and took two turns of the cable round the cross on the end of the gable. He pulled it tight, and the wire rose from among the gravestones and hung in a shallow curve over the hedge and up to the bedroom window.

While Tom cut the cable and led it into the Chapel through one of the windows, Septimus was working on the door. He stood on a chair and stapled a heavy elastic band to the inside of the frame an inch above the top of the door. Next, he took a small, low voltage switch from his pocket and screwed it to the door so that the elastic band fitted neatly over the knob, sufficiently tight for there to be no slack, but not tight enough to move the switch. He got down from his chair and opened the door slowly. The rubber band began to stretch, increasing its pull on the knob until with a little click the switch closed and the band slid off. He reset it and tried again. He tried four times, moving the door at different speeds. It worked each time.

'Very ingenious,' said Rosemary. 'Rector's patent burglar alarm. Did you invent it yourself?' She was sitting on the altar rail watching him.

'No,' he replied. 'As a matter of fact, I learnt how to do it in the war.'

It was a device used by the Yugoslavian Resistance to detonate a booby trap. He suddenly thought of the shattered rooms full of bits of men. But he did not tell her anything of that.

They connected the end of the wire to the two terminals on the switch, shut and bolted the bird grille, locked but did not bolt the door, and set the elastic band in position over the switch. They returned the ladder to its place under the tower and went back to the Rectory, It was almost dark now.

Rosemary and Tom followed Septimus up to the bedroom to see the final stages of the improvised alarm. What was left was very simple. Septimus simply wired a battery and a household door bell to the circuit and put them on the locker by his bed.

'Then if anyone opens the chapel door,' said Rosemary, 'the bell rings.'

'Yes,' he said, and with his penknife he completed the circuit across the terminals and the bell rang.

Tom spoke, and he was unusually serious.

'Squire, hadn't I better stay for the night? I mean—from what you say—there's two of them. You can't tackle two of them alone.'

'You ought to let us get Ted Harris and make it three of you,' said Rosemary. There was truth in what they said, and Septimus knew it. Tom might be a younger man, but he was only small and inexperienced in the dirty sort of fighting which might develop—if there was to be any fighting. And inside Septimus was a cold anger about Sir Handel. This was a personal matter and he was going to deal with it himself. He knew he was acting unwisely. A professional ought not to be personally involved. A professional would not take on two villains single-handed. But because of Sir Handel he refused to take notice of his own warning.

'Thanks, Tom,' he said. 'But I can deal with those two pasteboard rogues, and Rosemary would never forgive me if you got a black eye.'

'I wish you'd let us both stay,' she said. But he would not be persuaded, so Rosemary made coffee and they sat for a while talking. Rosemary was inquisitive. Over the last few days she had seen a country parson in a new light. Not just as 'the Rector', but as a man with a history and feelings and problems of his own. Perhaps it was the tension of possible action later, but Septimus found himself talking more freely than he usually did. He described what it had been like to pound a beat in the nineteen-twenties, and his war years parachuting into occupied Europe; the reasons why men took to crime, the differences between the amateur and the professional.

'Those two that are after the Cup,' said Rosemary, 'are they amateur or professional?'

Septimus was nonplussed for a moment, and then he realised why. This was the first job he had ever worked on before the crime was actually comitted.

'I don't know,' he said. 'If you called me in tomorrow—after they'd given the chapel a going over—I'd be able to tell you then.'

As they were on their way to the front door, Tom made a final attempt.

'Let me stay, Squire,' he pleaded. 'You could do with the help.'

But Septimus had made up his mind. Sir Handel had fought alone, and alone he would avenge the dog.

'Thanks, Tom, but it really isn't necessary. If I ever have any proper villains to deal with, I'll let you in on the act.'

He stood at the front door and watched the tail lights of Tom's car race down the drive. He was suddenly aware that he was alone. It was dark. The moon would not rise for another hour, and the clouds moved lazily across the stars. There was a whisper of breeze so that the dark trees rustled as if they were holding a quiet conversation. Septimus went to the gate leading into the churchyard, walking on the grass so that his feet did not crunch on the gravel. To his left he could see the trees of Danedyke Wood and the angular outline of the old tower against the lightness where the moon would rise over the North Sea. He searched the darkness, but his eyes could not identify the wire of his improvised burglar alarm. The opposition would not see it, and anyway he greatly doubted if they would realise its significance, even if they did see it. He went back to the house and made his preparations for the night. He changed into an old pair of grey slacks and a black roll-neck sweater and a pair of dark gym shoes. He went to his study and took his old truncheon from its place of honour on the wall. He slipped the cord over his wrist and gripped the handle and slapped the truncheon into his palm, smiling and remembering. He had only used it twice in the days when he had pounded a beat in London. Once on a very drunk Irish labourer, once to break a window. He was glad he had kept it as a memento. He would certainly use it if he had to.

He went to his bedroom and lay down fully-clothed, dragging the eiderdown over him. He took the book he was reading from the locker—Thomas Traherne's *Centuries of Meditation*.

'The corn was orient and immortal wheat which grew from

everlasting to everlasting . . .' The gentle world of Thomas Traherne seemed a long way away. He read for a while, then checked the bell once more with his pocket knife. He put out the light and was soon asleep.

When the bell woke him there was a faint gleam of moonlight coming through the bedroom window. He rolled over, un-screwed the terminal to silence the alarm, picked up his truncheon, and was standing on the bedside mat before the eiderdown had finished its slither to the floor. He looked out of the window, but there was nothing to indicate that someone had opened the Relic Chapel door. The moon was half ob-scured; garden, churchyard and church were all dark and silent. It was nearly three o'clock.

He went softly and swiftly down the stairs, unbolted the back door and stepped out into the night. There was a rustle of movement beside him in the dark porch. Instinctively he flung himself sideways, turning as he did so, raising the truncheon.

'It's only me, Squire.' Tom Barton's voice was a rather quavery whisper.

Septimus grinned in the darkness, and let the truncheon fall to his side.

'Tom, you old fool,' he said, 'I damn nearly clobbered you.'

'Yes. I know. But Rosemary and me, we thought you might need help. So I came back after I'd taken her home. I've been sitting in the porch.'

'I'm very grateful, Tom. But look. . . if there is a barney, don't expect it to be by Queensberry rules. Watch your eyes, and watch you don't get kicked in the crutch. Keep behind me and keep quiet. Have you got a weapon?'

'Squire,' whispered Tom, 'I've got the biggest damn span-ner you ever saw.'

Septimus moved toward the churchyard and it was a revelation to Tom that so big a man could move so quietly. One moment he was there outlined by the porch, next moment he was gone, a darker shadow moving among the greys and blacks of the night.

Septimus waited for a long time by the gate into the churchyard, staring into the gloom. Momentarily the half moon came from behind the clouds and the churchyard was bright, the gravestones like white rocks in a silver sea. The stonework of the church was the colour of pale honey, and they could see the dark shadow of the door leading into the Relic Chapel, but they could not tell whether it was open, nor whether there was anyone in the Chapel.

The moon plunged into cloud again, like the drawing of a curtain over the churchyard, and Tom felt a tug on his arm. The soundless shadow filled the gateway and flitted away along the side of the path. Tom followed as quietly as he could, his hand gripping the heavy spanner, his heart pounding. They crept along the grass until they were crouched under the side of a big box tomb a scant ten feet from the Chapel door.

The moon came out again, and its pale light surged like a silent tide over the churchyard, and the wall of the Chapel shone. The bird grille was open, its mesh casting a networked shadow on the stone wall. The door itself was dark and closed, dark as the shadows thrown by the buttresses down the sides of the Chapel.

Again the moon dipped behind a cloud, again darkness flooded over the churchyard, again Tom felt the Rector's hand on his arm.

Septimus moved softly toward the closed door. He waited on the step, listening, then he put a hand on the metal loop of the door handle. He heard a rustle in the shadows by the corner, and it was not Tom. He turned swiftly, stepping sideways, his hand gripping the truncheon, even as Tom cried out. In the darkness he saw a shadow, the silhouette of a man, dive at Tom, and then he dived himself, the truncheon raised. His mind was a thing apart from the automatic responses of his body, and he foresaw what was going to happen even before he landed on tiptoe beside the struggling heap on the path.

The setting up of the burglar alarm had been watched. The ambush was for both of them. He turned as he landed, not bothering about Tom now, trying to get out of the line of the attack which would surely come. But he was too late. He did not really feel the blow which struck him in the nape of the neck, although he was conscious that it happened. He was thinking 'Septimus, you bloody, bloody fool'. Then he saw a white light. Then he was engulfed in a roaring blackness.

8

The Morning After

Septimus groaned, opened his eyes, and found himself looking up into a face. A shiny pink face, a sinister one with the eyes too close together and a painted beard. A *painted* beard? He closed his eyes, shook his head—making it hurt even more than it was doing already—and then reopened his eyes. The face belonged to the effigy of Sir John Carruthers, lying self-satisfied and mocking on top of his tomb, and Septimus was on the Chapel floor beside the tomb, Tom Barton next to him, and dawn was seeping through the windows and it looked as if a bomb had hit the chapel. There were three gaping holes in the panels of the box base of Sir John's tomb. The chairs were pushed aside, piled higgledy-piggledy, some of them smashed. Most of the monuments had been wrenched from the walls. Septimus groaned again and sat up, rubbing the back of his head gingerly. The stone front of the altar had been wrenched open, making it look like a burst box. The tiles of the sanctuary were torn up in patches, and great areas of plaster had been levered from the walls.

Septimus caught hold of the edge of the tomb and dragged himself to his feet. He could feel grit under his fingers and someone had stubbed out a cigarette on the painted cushion upon which Sir John's head rested.

Tom was wriggling and moaning at his feet, and it took Septimus a moment to realise that Tom was not just coming back to consciousness. He was fully conscious already, but he was bound and gagged. Septimus knelt as quickly as his shaky state would allow and cut Tom's bonds with his penknife. He pulled him into a sitting position and took the gag from his mouth. For a while Tom could say nothing, the air rasping into his dry mouth. Septimus dragged him across the floor and propped him against the tomb, and then went stumbling across the rubble in search of water. The water cruet which was housed in the niche by the altar was smashed, and the base of the niche had been prised upward so that Septimus had to go through into the church itself to fetch the water cruet from beside the high altar. He poured half of it down Tom's throat and finished it off himself.

'Thanks, Rector,' croaked Tom, and then, 'They've made a right mess.'

'And that,' thought Septimus ruefully, contemplating the wreck of his Chapel, and refusing even to think of the wreck of his professional reputation, 'was the understatement of the twentieth century.'

'They didn't lay you out, Tom?'

Tom shook his head slowly. He was rubbing his ankles, wincing, almost crying with the pain of the restored circulation.

'There were two of them. The little one—the ginger one— jumped me. I suppose the big blighter with the beard clouted you. They tied me up, then they dragged us both inside. Then they brought tools in—crowbars and things—and they just took the place apart. Shouldn't think they've ever worked so hard in their lives.'

'Did they find anything?' asked Septimus.

'No, they didn't. And they had a row. The ginger one did all the talking. He seemed to think they should have waited. He seemed to be the leader—but he wasn't very well in charge, if you see what I mean. The other one, the big dark thug, he didn't say much. He didn't seem to like you, though. I think he'd have been glad of an excuse to do you in.'

The door into the churchyard opened and Rosemary stood in the pointed arch framed against the growing daylight.

'Oh, my God,' she said and came running to them, her feet slithering on the rubbish. 'Are you all right?'

'Nothing injured but our pride,' said Septimus. 'Walked straight into it we did. Never been so ashamed in all my life.' Then Rosemary was in Tom's arms, and Septimus was looking down at them, feeling very old, and wishing that his head did not ache quite so much.

'Nonsense, Charles,' said Septimus, and suiting action to sentiment he swung himself off the bed and on to the floor.

Summoned by Rosemary, Doctor Simmonds had arrived post haste at the Rectory, his peppery temper not of the best since he had missed his breakfast, and would now miss it altogether or be late for surgery. He had looked first at Tom and sent him home under the care of Rosemary. Then he had muttered and tutted over the swelling bruise on the back of Septimus's head, and finally announced that he must stay in bed.

'I'll not answer for the consequences if you don't,' he said frostily. 'You're a silly old goat, and any self-respecting man of your age would be in hospital with an injury like that.'

Septimus was standing on the bedside rug struggling into his trousers.

'Be reasonable, Charles,' he said. 'And don't shout at me. It makes my head ache. You know perfectly well it's Saturday and Jenny Jackson's getting married at one. Mary Crowle's practised the voluntary—I shouldn't have got this clout on the skull if she hadn't—and anyway, you know better than I with that damned clinic of yours that if I don't marry her soon it'll start to show.'

Charles Simmonds suddenly dropped his fierce pose and smiled.

'All right, Septimus. You'll have your own way, whatever I say. Make an honest woman of her and then come back to bed. And I'm glad our feathered friend didn't find the Cup, even if he did wreck the Chapel.'

'The question is,' said Septimus, 'is it there to be found if you look in the right place?'

Septimus could hear the tinny ringing tone of the Danedyke Garage phone for such a long time that he nearly hung up before Tom answered, his voice sleepy and bad-tempered.

'Tom. The Rector here. I just wanted to check something with you. When the rogues were taking the Relic Chapel apart you said that they quarrelled.'

'That's right,' said Tom, yawning.

'Gingerwhiskers said, "They should have waited." That was the way you told it to me. Did he say what they should have waited for?'

There was a silence while Tom thought about this.

'No, he didn't,' he said at length. 'He just said, "I told you we should have waited. It's no good groping around in the dark." Something like that.'

Jeremiah Clarke's 'Trumpet Voluntary' was echoing through the church and the wedding guests were crowding out of the north door in the wake of the bride and groom. Septimus left his surplice and stole in the vestry and went, as he had promised, to join the photographing outside the porch. He posed

as he was bidden, smiled as best he could, kissed Jenny—
which made everyone laugh—and then went to the Relic
Chapel.

He found Charles Simmonds surveying the damage.

'Just thought I'd see what we're going to have to pay for,'
said the doctor. 'And make sure you go home to bed.'

During the morning Rosemary with Mary Crowle had
routed out a protesting Harry Garner, insisting that for once
he did something to justify his position as churchwarden. The
three of them had done what they could to tidy the chapel, but
it still looked as if a bomb had hit it. Charles Simmonds stooped
by the altar, where the stone front gaped open. He thrust an
arm into the gap and brought out a piece of newspaper. It was
the *Daily Mail* for a day in September 1940, its front page
shouting urgent headlines about the Battle of Britain. The
priest and the doctor looked in silence at the yellow, fragile
paper.

'Your vandals are fools as well,' said Charles Simmonds.
'Even the shilling booklet about the church says this altar was
rebuilt in 1940.'

They went round the chapel together, mournfully surveying
the damage. It was indeed comprehensive. Nothing that might
conceivably conceal a hiding place had been left untouched.

'Not fools,' said the doctor at last. 'Just thorough. And it
looks, Septimus, as if we were on the wrong track. If John of
Danedyke ever hid his blessed Cup in this chapel, it isn't here
now. And isn't the gallant Colonel going to be pleased when
we get an estimate for the repairs?'

The door into the church opened and Ted Harris came in,
his uniform cap under his arm. He stood inside the doorway
and coughed self-consciously. Ted always felt faintly embar-
rassed when he had to deal with the Rector. You didn't know
where you were. There were parsons and there were police
officers. In Ted's opinion it was merely confusion to mix the
one with the other.

'Afternoon, Rector—doctor,' he said formally,'I was sorry

to hear about all this. 'He looked comprehensively round the chapel.' You know, Rector, you should have reported this . . .' He suddenly remembered that he was talking to an ex-Chief Inspector and his tone changed. 'You know that as well as I do, sir.' He was deferential and justly aggrieved.

'Yes, I know, Ted,' said Septimus. 'I'm sorry.'

Ted unbuttoned his uniform pocket and extracted notebook and pencil. 'I'll have to make a report, sir.'

Septimus stifled a sigh. He knew that Ted had to make a report. He also knew what it meant—twenty minutes of ponderous questions and laborious literary composition—and his head was aching abominably.

'Yes, Ted, I'm afraid you will. Sergeant Johnson in Wisbech will want to know all about this. So we might as well make ourselves comfortable.'

'I'm off,' said the doctor. 'Ted, when you've finished with the Rector, escort him across to the Rectory and see he goes to bed. I can't make him do it. Perhaps you can.' He made his escape by the door leading into the churchyard.

Twenty minutes later the report was done. Septimus had kept as much of the truth to himself as strict honesty would allow. He felt a little guilty about misleading Ted Harris, who was a good country copper, but he really couldn't face Sergeant Johnson tramping around and detecting all over the place. As a result Ted got the impression that he was dealing with some sort of hooligan treasure hunt. The policeman stood up at length, putting his notebook away and buttoning the pocket.

'Well,' he said, 'I reckon they must have been locals, Rector. Though I'm hanged if I can think who I've got on my patch that you could call a tearaway. There's young Gordon Bates—that's Ned Bates's eldest—but Gordon's not a tearaway. Not really. He's only elevenpence in the shilling. For all he pinched the Colonel's turkeys . . .' He stood, pondering the petty villainies of the fen.

Septimus was startled. Ted Harris would never make his

name in the C.I.D. but when he talked about local crime he was worth listening to. He probably knew as much about what went on under the placid surface of village life as the Rector and the doctor added together.

'A local job, Ted?' he asked. 'Why?'

'Aye. Well. It's like this, Rector. You know old Jack up at the Mill? Well. He knows he's the biggest poacher in the county. And I know he's the biggest poacher in the county. So do you, Rector, come to that. Well, The Colonel's been on to me about his pheasants. And Jack hasn't been up before a magistrate for nigh on four years. Well, I reckoned he was out last night. Just something I heard in the Bluebell when I was off duty. So last night I was out half the night looking for old Jack, and there wasn't a foreigner's car parked within half a mile of the church. I'll swear to that. There's only the Lynn Road and the Wisbech Road and the three lanes, and I cycled down 'em all—and more than once. So whoever it was did this chapel—he must have walked.'

There was a long silence while Septimus gazed at the policeman with unblinking blue eyes. Ted Harris shifted uncomfortably.

'You all right, Rector?'

'Yes, of course, Ted. I was just thinking what an intelligent deduction that was and what an advantage it is to have a copper who really knows his patch and the villains in it.'

Ted blushed and smiled. Praise from a Chief Inspector was praise indeed—even if he was an ex-Chief Inspector, and a clergyman into the bargain.

'Well. Thank you, sir,' he said. 'That's right nice of you. And now I've to do what Doctor Simmonds said—see you across to the Rectory. Promise you'll go to bed, sir?'

Despite his weariness and the pain in his head, it was some little time before Septimus managed to go to sleep; his mind was too occupied with the significance of what Ted Harris had said.

Of course it had not been a local job. It had been Ginger-whiskers and the man who had driven the Jaguar, and there was nothing local about them. Even so, Ted had put an unerring finger on something that Septimus ought to have seen for himself. He and Tom had been ambushed—which meant that one or other of the villains had watched them erecting the burglar alarm. And that meant a position from which the churchyard could be watched. He called to mind the geography of the thing. The most likely spot was the old lookout tower in Danedyke Wood. About half a mile down the Dane-dyke there was a track connecting with the Wisbech Road. You could drive to the bottom of it, leave the car, walk along the Danedyke, and keep the churchyard under observation from the top of the old tower. It would be a bit of a sweat, but you could also carry the heavy tools which had been used for the assault on the Chapel down the Danedyke and store them in the wood until you wanted them. He did not doubt that that was how it had been done. He was tempted to get up and go straight across to Danedyke Wood. But the villains would long ago have evacuated the tower. It would do later. So he slept.

He awoke feeling greatly refreshed, and lay a moment, gratefully savouring the blessed truth that his head had stopped hurting. The church clock struck six and he sat up, wincing suddenly with pain. He had the great grand-daddy of all stiff necks. He climbed out of bed. Apart from the stiff neck, he was feeling very much better. He was also feeling very hungry, and he suddenly remembered that he had eaten nothing for twenty-four hours.

He went down to the kitchen and cooked himself a mixed grill. He did it carefully and well. The years of living alone had turned him into a good cook when he cared to bother. When he had finished the meal he washed the dishes and took his coffee into the study. Then he went and dressed as he had done on the previous evening, but instead of the truncheon he took a big rubber torch. As a weapon it was nearly as effective as a truncheon—and you couldn't get a light out of a truncheon.

It was nearly dark, the clouds heavy, but with lightness over the sea where the clouds came to an end. There was a stiff breeze rustling in the trees, sending leaves whispering along the paths.

He went out of the back door, across the overgrown garden, through the spinney where he had found Sir Handel and so out into the open field. For five minutes he stood motionless gazing at the lookout tower outlined against the gathering night. He was not aware of the stillness of his standing; it was simply that the long years of training told. At last he moved— soundlessly—along the side of the sparse hedge which best concealed him from the tower. The worst noise of his passage came from a rabbit which neither scented nor heard him until he was only five feet away. It then fled with a thumping of hind feet and a loud rustling of dry gorse. Septimus stopped in his tracks, feeling the rate of his heartbeat increase, feeling suddenly vulnerable. It took him a moment to identify the fear, and then he relaxed. His body was expecting bullets out of the darkness! But that all belonged to the distant past. Whatever Gingerwhiskers did—even supposing he was in the tower, which was extremely unlikely—he certainly wouldn't open fire with an automatic.

So Septimus came to the Danedyke Wood. He skirted the scanty trees of the copse and went to the bank of the Danedyke itself and stood looking down at the smooth dark water, waiting, motionless as a post, waiting to see if there was any hint of movement in the wood itself.

The minutes crawled by and still he stood. Five . . . ten minutes.

A fish rose with a sudden 'plop' in the Danedyke, and Septimus watched the rings circling outward across the oily water. Twelve minutes. A fox barked across the fen, and far away by Danedyke Saint Peter a farm dog barked in reply. The wind rustled the trees, and he could smell the salt in the wind. Twenty minutes, a badger came blundering down the path by the dyke. It paused twelve feet away from him, sniffing the air suspiciously. But the wind was wrong, so that Septimus could smell badger rather than the other way round. The badger snorted and trotted on down the path, and Septimus sighed, easing cramped limbs. He was alone in Danedyke Wood.

9
The 'Grace of Wisbech'

Although he was sure that he was alone in Danedyke Wood, Septimus waited for a long moment before he entered the doorway of the old tower. It was black, and he was conscious of himself silhouetted against the greyness of the night.

He switched on his torch and went inside.

The base of the tower was empty, nothing but a bare rectangle of rough stone with the unguarded steps going round the four sides. He swept his torch across the broken floor, looking for signs of recent occupation. There were only an empty cigarette packet—but it had certainly been thrown down since last it rained, because the tower was roofless and the packet dry.

He went up the steps, walking cautiously because of their erratic size, conscious of the absence of a guard rail. At the top he came out on a narrow walkway—really the top of the walls themselves, with a broken parapet on the outside and a sheer, unguarded drop on the inside. He moved slowly round the wall, picking his way, unwilling to use the torch in such an exposed position. He went first to the side of the tower which looked back over the church and the village. Here there was rather more parapet, and he crouched down behind it, searching the flags with his torch. There were cigarette ends which had recently been crushed against the stone, and they were of the same brand as the empty packet. He stood up, switching off the torch. Over the top of the parapet he could see the outline of the church and the lights and roofs of the village. The street lamp by the telephone kiosk cast its beams into the churchyard, lighting up some of the gravestones.

His hunch had been right. Clearly the watch had been kept from here. It was from here that the setting up of the burglar alarm had been observed, and then the alarm had been used as a trap to ensure uninterrupted possession of the chapel—a desperate gamble, but a well-planned one as far as it went, and forced on them by his own activities. And what would they do now—if anything? What more could they do? And did the Cup still exist, or was the whole business just foolishness? The moon came from behind the clouds and the muddled outlines of church and village took on perspective, the roofs of differing shades, grey and blue and silver, the gravestones white specks against the dark grass.

He turned and looked toward the sea. The tower stood on a slight rise in the flat ground, and the extra few feet gave it command of limitless distances. Far to the south, orange against the night, he could see the lights of Wisbech, with the lights of King's Lynn like an echo to the east. Due east were the featureless marshes, scored across them the silver line of the Danedyke, beyond them the shimmering sea itself, the moon catching the wavetops. The tide was out. To the north lay the Wash, a tangle of shining water channels, sand banks, mud-flats, stretching away and away into the night.

Septimus was struck as he had been in the past, when he first accepted the living, by the loneliness of Danedyke Saint Mary. Mostly it seemed to live in the twentieth century. But that was only a surface pretence. There would come a moment when the mask slipped and you realised that it stood—as it always had done since the days of the Abbot John, since before John, when the Danes came with fire and sword sailing over the shallow seas, since the very first huddled settlements among the marshes—as an outpost, a tiny human defiance in a limitless emptiness dominated for ever by the sea and the great winds swooping out of the east.

He moved round the tower again until he was looking down at the placid waters of the Danedyke beneath the trees of the wood. It ran nearly straight for ten miles, its southern end joining the river north of Wisbech, its northern end running into the Wash. It was both land drain and sea wall. Originally built to hold back the encroaching sea, later in its long history it had been turned into a waterway and used both for transport and to drain the rich, black fen country.

The moon was momentarily bright so that Septimus could see the path running along the bank beside the water and disappearing among the trees surrounding the tower. There was something silver glinting on the bank. Septimus fixed its position in his mind before the moon went in again and the bright gleam vanished.

He went down the steps and searched along the path until he found the object. It was an empty sardine tin, the oil in it still fresh. Holding the tin in his hand, Septimus flashed his torch down the steep bank of the dyke toward the water. Below where he was standing the reeds were crushed and the bank muddy with footprints. A boat had been moored to the bank—and recently. He stood a moment, considering, the sardine tin forgotten between his fingers. A moored boat could mean everything—or nothing. Certainly the Danedyke was used by pleasure craft in the summer, although because it was dull and straight and its high banks precluded all view, it never carried a fraction of the busy, thronging traffic that used the river. A late holiday-maker—or a base of operations for Gingerwhiskers and his colleague? Septimus was morally certain that the latter was the truth. It would make such a perfect base, and it explained such a lot—how they were able to get to the church without their car ever being seen in the village, for one thing. Here on the edge of the wood a boat could lie concealed for a week. No one could physically see it at all unless they actually walked along the bank of the Dane-dyke. And anyone who did see it would merely conclude that it was being used by someone having a late holiday. The church could be kept under observation. It would be relatively easy to carry heavy tools to the Relic Chapel. And for quick lines of communication, a car could be left at the bottom of the lane which ran down to the dyke half a mile away in the Wisbech direction. It was not until he got back to the Rectory that he discovered he was still carrying the sardine tin.

'The Lord be with you,' said the Rector, looking at the ill-matched sizes of Saint Mary's choir and wondering how it was that little Georgie Maydew always managed to make his surplice look like a badly whitewashed horsecollar.

'And with thy spirit,' the choir replied in an assortment of squeaky trebles and rusty basses. Then the usual babble of conversation burst in the crowded vestry.

Septimus took off his surplice and went round the outside of the church to greet his congregation as they came trickling out of the porch. There was more than the usual domestic and village chatter. People were excited about the damage to the Relic Chapel, solicitous about the damage to their Rector, and Colonel Carruthers was very angry about what he called the 'desecration' of his ancestor's tomb. Septimus answered questions and made soothing noises and in the middle of it managed to catch Rosemary Horton and invite her and Tom across to the Rectory for a glass of sherry.

He was decanting the sherry when they arrived, Tom

uncommonly tidy in his blue Sunday suit. They sat sipping sherry while Septimus told them of his explorations of the previous night and the deductions he had made.

'So if you were a villain, Tom,' he concluded, 'where would you hire a cabin cruiser late in the autumn?'

'Wisbech,' said Tom immediately, then sat a moment, thinking, his arm round Rosemary's shoulder. Because of his sideline in repairs to marine engines, Tom was something of an expert on local cabin cruisers and boat yards.

'There's only three places really,' he said. 'All the rest have closed down for the season—sorting out the battle damage now the hordes have gone home. There's Macklings. They're the biggest. They've still got a few cruisers out. One of them ran a big end last Tuesday and I had to drive halfway to Peter-borough . . . So have Jones and Stott. And there's Joe Burton up by the bridge. He's only got a couple of boats, but he tries to keep them on the go all the time—to help out with the fish and chips.'

'Is there likely to be anyone in the yards on a Sunday after-noon?' Septimus asked.

'Oh, I should think so. They do a lot of their work with casual labour—garage people like me. You thinking of going for a shufty, Squire? We'll come with you if you like.'

'Fine,' said Septimus. 'I'll pick you up at two-thirty.'

He saw them off, refusing Rosemary's pressing invitation to lunch.

At the door he said, 'By the way Tom, have you got any technical manuals for Jaguars in your garage?'

'Some,' said Tom, surprised.

'Well be a good chap and look up the width of the wheel track and the tyre size of a nineteen sixty-five two-and-a-half litre. Can you do that?'

'Yes,' said Tom. 'What do you want it for?'

'Wait and see,' said Septimus.

Septimus collected Tom and Rosemary punctually at two

thirty, and they drove out of the village on the Wisbech Road, the three of them in a row on the bench seat of the landrover. Septimus turned off the main road down the unsurfaced track which led to the Danedyke. They bumped along for three-quarters of a mile until the lane ended abruptly at right-angles to the high bank of the dyke, separated from it by a broken five-bar gate. Septimus left the landrover in the middle of the track and climbed down. In front of the gate the track widened into a muddy turning space, and there were many old tyre marks. Mostly they belonged to tractors, but there was one set belonging to a car, several times repeated, and more modern than any of the others.

Rosemary and Tom climbed down from the landrover and stood watching him as he took a steel tape from his pocket and set about measuring the width of the track of the car.

'Five foot two,' he said, looking up at Tom.

'That fits your Jag, Squire,' said Tom. 'Mind you, I bet it fits half a dozen other cars as well. Probably fit a nineteen twenty-three Daimler.'

'Villains don't drive nineteen twenty-three Daimlers,' said Septimus. 'Not unless they're in the vintage car business. A six inch radial. Does that fit the Jaguar?'

'Six by nineteen,' said Tom. 'Yes, it does. Sherlock Treloar will now whip out his magnifying glass and crawl across the library floor muttering.'

Septimus stood up, grinning, looking boyish, so that Rosemary was surprised by an inward urge to stroke his mane of greying hair.

'No doubt about it,' he said. 'A nineteen twenty-three Daimler driven by a maverick duchess addicted to the bottle.' He was morally certain that he had just been measuring the tracks of the blue-grey Jaguar.

There was no one in the office at Macklings, but there was the sound of hammering coming from the cavernous boatshed. They parked the landrover on the quay alongside the silent flotilla of gaily-painted boats, and Tom led the way into the shed.

There was a man in greasy overalls hammering at a marine engine chocked up on a bench. Tom exchanged technical pleasantries, and then introduced him to the Rector as 'Fred'.

'The Rector's got something to ask you,' he said, and then fell silent, suddenly wondering how Septimus would handle his questions without being indiscreet.

Septimus slipped easily into his bumbling, vaguely benevolent, country parson act, to Rosemary's total astonishment. He looked the same—he was the same big man in a baggy tweed suit. But he had suddenly become a garrulous, well-intentioned backwoods cleric without an idea in his head more complicated than choosing the hymns for the harvest festival service. Septimus hoped that Fred would excuse him because it really was all rather complicated. And also he hoped that Fred would not mind being called Fred, because that was how Tom Barton had introduced him. And if his surname was Bates, he would still call him Fred, because Fred was a Christian name, and it was right and proper for a clergyman to use a Christian name, wasn't it?

The performance went on for quite five minutes and Rosemary and Tom listened with absorbed fascination. It really was brilliant. Out of the flood of words there emerged a clearcut, totally convincing, and entirely fictitious story.

It seemed that two gentlemen, one large and dark with a beard, one small and ginger with a moustache, names unknown but described in detail, had visited Saint Mary's Danedyke. They had been having a late holiday together in a cabin cruiser hired in Wisbech. They were no doubt architects, since they had been most interested in the church, and the Rector had spent a happy hour with them displaying its beauties. After they had gone he had discovered that they had put no less than £10 in the offertory box for Church Restoration. It must have been them, because the Rector was most careful to empty the box daily on account of the theft and vandalism which was so sadly rife in these dissolute days—as he was sure Fred would agree.

'So I wanted to thank them for their kindness,' he ended. 'I wrote them a letter. I said how refreshing it was to find such generosity. It quite restores one's faith to discover that even today we may entertain angels unawares. I enclosed a picture postcard—a coloured picture postcard—of the angel roof. It's almost unique, you know. Some say it's even better than March. But when I came to address the envelope . . . Of course! Silly me! I didn't know their names or addresses. But then dear Thomas came to my aid—Tom's Vicar's warden you know, and a very good one if I may say so. No, I won't spare your blushes, Tom. You are a good warden. What should we do about the rotor scythe if it wasn't for you? The church-yard's never been so well cared for since you took over. Where was I? Oh yes. So Tom suggested we might trace the address by finding where they hired the boat. As he pointed out it was almost certain to have been in Wisbech. So here we are, Fred! Making our detective enquiries. "Private dicks", I think the phrase is in Miss Agatha Christie. Or is it "Private eye"? I really forget.'

Rosemary suddenly snorted with mirth and hastily turned her snort into a coughing fit.

Fred Bates led them across to the office and looked up the bookings. There were five cruisers out, but for three of them the dates were wrong, and of the other two, one had been hired to six teenagers from whom Mr Mackling had extracted a double deposit, and the other to a young couple with a baby in a carry-cot.

As they drove away from Macklings through the sleepy, Sunday afternoon town, Rosemary collapsed into peels of laughter, her head thrown back against Tom's shoulder. At last she sat up, wiping her eyes on Tom's handkerchief.

'What a performance!' she said. 'You sounded like a country parson in a farce. "Private dick" in Agatha Christie!' She collapsed again in mirth.

'Bad example,' said Tom. 'That's what you are. Never thought I'd live to hear it. All those fibs. I shall jag in the churchwarden bit and join the Methodists.'

'Parsons and coppers,' said Septimus, his eyes on the road. 'They're the best liars. Only way to keep up with the great British Public.'

At Jones and Stott they had to knock up Mr Stott from his Sunday afternoon sleep in the modern bungalow across the road from the boatyard. At first he was inclined to be bad-tempered and uncooperative, but with a combination of flattery and the obsequious eagerness of a Saint Bernard dog hoping for a bone, Septimus managed to smooth the ruffled feathers.

Jones and Stott had three boats out, and none of them fitted.

There was nothing at all to indicate Joe Burton's boatyard. In fact, it was not really a yard at all. They went down an alley beside the fish-and-chip shop from which Joe made most of his living. At the back of the shop was a big and beautifully kept garden running down to the river, and at the riverside a couple of cruisers were moored. They ran Joe to earth in a shed at the bottom of the garden. He was a wizened little man, brown as a berry, and doing something with chrysanthemum tubers.

He and Tom had a chat about a crankshaft that needed grinding and then Septimus started on his fable for the third time. At the end of it Joe Burton took the stumpy briar from between his broken teeth and pointed through the window of the shed.

'*Grace of Wisbech*,' he said. 'My fourberther. Chap with ginger whiskers from London and his mate—big dark chap—surly-like. Name of Jones.' He put the pipe back between his teeth and lit it, sending clouds of acrid blue smoke billowing through the shed.

'Fortnight ago,' he said, 'hired her for a month. Paid the lot in advance. Jones—him with the ginger whiskers—brought her in yesterday and his pal picked him up in a blue Jaguar. Said some business had turned up and they'd got to go. But they'd be back, so I wasn't to think they'd finished with the cruiser.'

'Have you got an address?' asked Tom.

'Course I've got an address,' said the old man scornfully. He took a battered notebook from his pocket.

'Here it is. H. D. Jones, 23a Lampeter Road, Camberwell, S.E.5.'

They thanked the old man and left him to his foul pipe and his tubers, but in the doorway Septimus turned back.

'Mr Burton,' he said. 'When my friends do return I'd be most obliged if you would keep my little secret. It's a beautiful picture of our angel roof, and I would like Mr Jones to get it as a splendid surprise. After all, it was such a lovely surprise that he and his friend gave me—no less than £10 for the restoration fund. We shall spend it on the bells, you know.' He looked like a cow contemplating a rich meadow.

The old man put his hand into his pocket.

'Mum's the word, Reverend,' he said. 'And here's a couple of bob for the bells.'

They drove away from the fish-and-chip shop in pregnant silence until Septimus started to hum a tuneless version of the Hallelujah Chorus from *The Messiah*. Rosemary looked side-long at him. 'Mr Treloar,' she said, 'I think you're a wicked old man.'

He smiled, changing gear, his eyes on the bend in the road.

'I've got a florin for the bells,' he said, 'and if the pubs were open at this God-forsaken hour on a Sunday I'd buy a bottle of champagne to celebrate.'

'You think you'll find Gingerwhiskers in Camberwell?' asked Tom.

'If 23a Lampeter Road exists I'll put ten quid in the restoration fund myself,' said Septimus.

'Well anyway, S. E.5 is Camberwell,' said Tom, slightly aggrieved.

'But don't you see the point, my children? Don't you see why we should be drinking champagne and guzzling oysters, and I should be telling you the history of my life and all the triumphs of my years of detection with tears in my eyes and a quaver in my voice?'

'No,' said Tom. 'Not if it's not 23a Lampeter Road.'

'You're an oil-soaked cockney halfwit and you don't deserve to marry Rosemary. In fact I think I shall marry her myself. Don't you see, mes enfants? Horrible Gingerwhiskers has kept his options open. He means to come back for the *Grace of Wisbech*. Not only did they not find the Cup—which we knew already. But—the little darlings—they think it's still there. They're going to have another go, and that gives me another chance to clobber them.'

They passed the de-restriction sign and Septimus accelerated and started to sing again. The tuneless Hallelujah Chorus wafted away into the unoffending afternoon.

10

Buckshot Johnny

Nothing happened for several days, except that on the following Wednesday Septimus received the expected letter from Sam Burroughs. He sat over his frugal breakfast weighing the long envelope in his hand. It was marked 'Private and Confidential' and he started to sing again. The tuneless Hallelujah Chorus and the official stationery brought back a flood of memories of the pokey office in New Scotland Yard.

Inside was a short, caustic and slightly indecent letter from Sam, which ended '. . . so if you love me, Septic, burn the enclosure.' Septimus turned to the enclosure and very soon saw why Sam wanted it burned.

It was a document of such privacy and frankness that Sam Burroughs was risking both job and reputation by sending it to a country parson who, even if he had once been a member of the force, certainly now had no manner of entitlement to such information.

Septimus gulped, realising with a surge of emotion how highly the cynical Sam must hold his friendship. But then Sam always had been one to take a calculated risk. His mind skated back into the past, and he remembered standing behind a police car, a loud hailer in his hand, watching Sam running for a doorway, the bullets fired by a cornered gunman screeching off the cobbles behind his heels. Sam had got to the doorway, and so they had arrested Buckshot Johnny. Edwin Bates had been his real name, Septimus remembered. But the underworld with its passion for melodrama called him Buckshot Johnny because his favourite weapon was a sawn-off shotgun. That had been a very long time ago and both he and Sam had been a lot younger. Johnny had been sent down for a great number of years, and he could not remember how long the sentence had been. He sat for a moment, frowning, trying to remember, but then he put the question away. He must not live in the past, that way lay melancholy ruin.

He turned to the enclosure. It was one page of typed quarto, and consisted of an appraisal of the market for famous stolen works of art.

There were three suspected fences: one in London, one in Paris and one in New York. There were six suspected purchasers whose combined estimated wealth ran to nine figures. Two were Americans—an oil magnate, and a manufacturer of candy living in California. There was a cockney-born owner of a shipping fleet who also owned a Greek island. There was a Swedish manufacturer of machine tools, an Italian Count of long descent whose titles ran to two lines, and finally there was a Frenchman living in Switzerland of whom very little seemed to be known except that he was a leading authority on Impressionist painting and had narrowly escaped a lengthy prison sentence over a stolen Gauguin.

Septimus sat for a while pondering the phenomenon of a man amassing a collection of stolen works of art. Presumably you kept the stolen pieces separate from your honest collection. And when you showed the honest collection to your friends, were you thinking 'Ah! If you only knew what I've got behind that locked door, you'd envy me then'? Did you sit and gloat in secret? And what did you do about your stolen collection in your will? And why did these hoards of stolen treasure so rarely come to light?

He looked again at the list. What an extraordinary thing it was that five of the six men were of unblemished reputation and ran businesses of known probity. Men who would scorn to steal with their own hands, but who would yet buy works of art knowing them to be stolen. He tried to imagine the sort of conversation they would have with some corrupt dealer in an expensive apartment in Paris or New York. The way the stark realities would be avoided; the urbane jokes; the carefully chosen phraseology. 'Of course there are two in the Louvre, but I fear they are not for sale.' Then the extravagant delight over the stolen object itself, the use of the elegant phrases of appreciation, the bland ignoring of corruption and theft when perhaps some wretched museum attendant was lying in hospital with a fractured skull, his wife weeping by his bedside. If only such people had imagination! If only they could see the stark reality that lay behind the sophisticated collecting.

He gave up the speculation, committed the digest to memory, burnt both it and Sam's letter and went across to school.

Rosemary Horton had made a fine model of the Holy Land in the sand tray, and Septimus spent a happy half-hour discussing with her seven-year-olds—half of whom had never seen a hill—the story of the Good Samaritan, and how the road really did 'go down', as the Bible said it did, from Jerusalem to Jericho. Septimus knew the road from personal experience, so he talked about it rather well. He did not think it necessary to tell Class 2 about the dead bodies he had seen on it, nor the fact that he had last driven down it in an armoured car.

When he walked back into the Rectory the phone was ringing, and it was an emergency. It was Mrs Jackson from the Home Farm, an agitated Mrs Jackson. Harry Garner had turned the tractor over.

'He's hurt real bad, Rector. We've got him in the parlour, but Jack says will you come?'

Septimus slipped easily into an old routine. Was Harry bleeding badly?

No. He just seemed to be crushed like. But he was unconscious.

Well, they were to cover him with a blanket and on no account to move him.

Had they rung the doctor?

Yes. Doctor Simmonds was on his way.

Had they dialled 999 and got an ambulance?

No.

Well, they were to do that next. Septimus had already done the sum in his head about how long it would take an ambulance to get from Wisbech. It was very probable that Charles Simmonds had done the same sum, but it was better to ask for an ambulance twice than not at all.

Had they rung the police?

Yes. Ted Harris was on his way.

Had anyone told Mrs Garner?

No.

Well, nobody was to do that until he got there. Septimus was thinking of Mrs Garner's heart, and he wanted speech with Charles Simmonds before anyone got near Mrs Garner with a tale of disaster.

He put the phone down and went to the garage for the land-rover.

The rest of the day was a muddle of urgent practicalities and a steady defusing of overwrought emotions.

Rosinante was already parked by the dairy as he drove into the yard of the Home Farm sending the free-range hens scattering in panic. A weeping Mrs Jackson took him into the parlour where Charles Simmonds was kneeling by the silent, blanket-covered Harry Garner.

The doctor shooed Mrs Jackson out of her own parlour.

'How is he?' asked Septimus.

'He's got about four broken ribs and a broken collar bone. But they'll mend. It's his back I'm worried about.'

The ambulance came swinging into the yard, its bell ringing dramatically. Doctor Simmonds supervised the moving of Harry into the ambulance while Septimus set Mrs Jackson to making tea for all and sundry as the best way of calming her down. Then he had to deal with John Jackson, the farmer and owner of the tractor, who was insistent that he had always forbidden Harry to use the tractor at the bottom end of the Dyke Meadow.

'It's too damned steep, Rector. I've told him, and I've told him again. But you know what Harry is, Rector.'

Then Charles Simmonds came back from phoning the hospital in Wisbech, and they went together in Rosinante to break the news to Mrs Garner.

Septimus got the actual job of telling her, while the doctor waited in the car.

'If we arrive on the doorstep together,' the doctor said, 'her heart'll stop from sheer fright before she even knows what's happened.'

Mrs Garner took the bad news better than Septimus had expected, and then the doctor came in and he had to make the difficult decision as to whether Mrs Garner could be allowed to go to the hospital to see Harry.

He decided she could, issued pills and instructions, and took both Mrs Garner and Septimus back to the Home Farm.

Septimus drove Mrs Garner into Wisbech in the landrover because Charles Simmonds had to go on to another seriously-ill patient.

They waited at the hospital for four weary hours while Harry was in the operating theatre, and then by his bed as he lay unconscious, his thin face brown against the white pillow.

It was nearly four o'clock when Harry fluttered into consciousness like a brown moth coming hesitantly toward a light.

It was going to be all right after all.

They sat for a quarter of an hour and then left Harry to sleep, and Septimus drove Mrs Garner home, made her a cup of tea and left her watching a children's programme on television.

As he turned the landrover into the Rectory drive Rosemary Horton came along the pavement, her arms full of flowers for the church. He stopped with the front wheels in the gateway and told her about Harry.

'Yes, I know,' she said, 'Tom told me at lunchtime. Fison's traveller told him. Is Harry going to be all right?'

'Looks like it,' said Septimus, and then because he had missed his lunch and was hungry and because it had been an emotional day, 'Silly old fool. More than he deserves.'

The phone was ringing once again as he walked in the front door after putting the landrover away.

He went irritably to the study and picked up the receiver. He had spent all the damned day doing what he could about a near tragedy which ought never to have happened in the first place. He was tired and he was hungry. And the blasted phone ought to be banned by law.

'Septimus Treloar,' he snarled.

'Rector! I've caught you at last. I've tried three times during the day, but there was no reply.'

Septimus thought, 'Of course there was no reply you bone-headed nit, whoever you are. With that bloody fool Harry

Garner turning over a perfectly stable tractor, what the hell do you expect? 'What he said was,' Yes. I've been out all day. Who's speaking?'

'Cedric Empson,' said the metallic voice of the telephone.

'Cedric Empson?' Septimus was conscious of the distaste in his own voice. There was no Cedric Empson in the parish of Danedyke Saint Mary, and he wanted his tea.

'Yes,' said the telephone, 'librarian of Gloucester College.' Septimus's voice went sharply up in tone as he changed gear.

'I'm terribly sorry, Mr Empson. I've been coping all day with a farming accident, and you took me by surprise. What can I do for you?'

The voice at the other end of the anonymous line was excited, and Septimus had a sudden vision of little Mr Empson dancing from one foot to the other in the wide spaces of Gloucester College library.

'Rector! I promised you should be the first to know, and I've been trying to tell you all day. Rector . . . Mr Treloar . . . the Danedyke Gospel. We've found the missing picture!'

'You've what?' Septimus's explosion of surprise was violent enough to be some sort of reward for the little librarian.

'Yes. We've found it. We have indeed. Very simple really. Childishly simple—and I really ought to have guessed. After all, that's what librarians are for, and I've never had much opinion of eighteenth-century bookbinders. The page had been misbound, Mr Treloar. It was in volume twelve. Bound in at the end as if it were a colophon. You remember—the Gospels are in volume six? It really is a remarkable picture. Indeed it makes a very good colophon. I can almost forgive the binder—now we've found it.'

'Tell me about it,' said Septimus.

'Well, as you remember, it's part of the twenty-fourth chapter of Saint Matthew. There's a picture. An illumination to the beginning of verse fifteen. It's the piece about the abomination of desolation. You remember it, Mr Treloar?'

Septimus did not reply for a moment as the words from the fourth text quoted on John of Danedyke's gravestone ran through his mind.

'When ye therefore shall see the abomination of desolation, spoken of by Daniel the prophet, stand in the holy place (whoso readeth, let him understand).'

'Yes,' he said. 'Go on, Mr Empson, I remember.'

'Well. It's a remarkable picture. A picture of a tomb. And it's so modern. So Renaissance. Professor Hakenbaum will be thrilled. I've never seen anything like it—except the other illustrations in the Gospels of course. It looks like a Tudor tomb. There's the usual stone box with an Elizabethan worthy lying on top—just like half the wool merchant tombs in the Cotswold churches. He's got his head on a sort of pillow . . . not a pillow really . . . more like one of those wooden box kneelers with an upholstered top. But the extraordinary thing is that there appears to be a sort of door in the side of the kneeler. And if you look at it through a magnifying glass there's a figure coming out of the door. And the figure is Lazarus. Just the same as the Lazarus in the Saint John illustration. Exactly the same, only of course much, much smaller. It's so well done that you can see the cup he is carrying quite clearly.'

He went on talking, but Septimus was not listening.

Sir John Carruthers' tomb! He could see it in his mind's eye. The stiff figure, looking not like a reclining man, but like a statue laid on its side, its head propped on a stone pillow. Of course it looked like that, because that was what it was. He had never examined the figure closely, but he had always taken it for granted that figure and pillow were carved in one piece— as a modern sculptor would carve them. But perhaps that was not the way of the sixteenth century. If the figure was carved separately and laid into position on top of the tomb . . . then there was no reason why the boxlike pillow should be carved from the solid. If it was hollow . . . He thanked the librarian as warmly as he could, unwilling to sound abrupt, but eager to

95

ring off and go across to the church, all thought of his hunger now forgotten.

'Before you go, Rector, there is one other thing. I'm sorry I couldn't keep my promise about Mr Jones—to let you know before him, the Professor's research assistant. You see . . . I couldn't. Not really. It was Mr Jones who found the missing page. As a matter of fact I suggested the possibility to him— eighteenth-century binders being what they were, and he came over and started to go through the Madresfield Papers page by page.'

'When did he find it?' asked Septimus swiftly.

'About eleven o'clock this morning. I'd been out of the library—for a cup of coffee as a matter of fact—and I'd just come back, and I saw the page over his shoulder. He didn't hear me come back into the library, and I've an idea he wasn't too pleased that I saw it. I think he wanted to keep it a secret. I can't imagine why.'

'I expect he wanted to tell the Professor before anyone else knew about it,' said Septimus.

He thanked the librarian and rang off.

He collected a couple of cold chisels, a screwdriver and a hammer from his workshop and went across to the church.

As he went in at the north door, Rosemary Horton was coming down the aisle carrying a watering can.

'Going to do some tidying up in the Chapel?' she asked, seeing the tools in his hands.

'Yes,' he lied, realising as he did so that he wanted no company for what he was about to do.

He went into the Relic Chapel, closing the door behind him.

It was so obvious that the effigy of Sir John Carruthers had been carved in an upright position and then laid on its side that he could only wonder how he had not seen it before. Even the complex folds of Sir John's gown hung as they would have done had he been standing up.

The pillow on which his head lay was a stone box about fifteen inches wide, a foot long and nine inches deep. Its top was carved and painted red, an upholstered red velvet pillow carved in stone, with carved golden tassels hanging from the corners. The box upon which the pillow rested was painted brown and framed as if its side panels were made of wood.

Septimus stooped over the box, his head close to Sir John's. The blind painted eyes stared into his, mocking him as always.

He tapped the box.

It was hollow.

The one hollow space which the opposition had not investigated when they took the Chapel apart.

With his pencil torch he examined the box closely. The sides were let into a frame, with a bevelled fillet like glass puttied into a window — except that all was painted brown.

He put the blade of the screwdriver on to the fillet and tapped the handle smartly, using his clenched fist as a mallet. The edge of the screwdriver slipped, bringing with it brown paint and a powdering of white. The fillet was clearly some sort of cement. He took the smallest of the cold chisels and started to chip at the fillet. It came away easily, like old putty in an unpainted window, and the panel beneath it was made of slate.

When he had chipped out the fillet all the way round he got out his pocket knife and thrust it into the crack between the edge of the slate and the frame, moving it backwards and forwards, levering gently. The panel seemed to shift, and he pressed harder.

With a 'crack' which was loud in the quiet chapel the knife blade broke.

'Damn!' said Septimus.

He took the screwdriver, put the edge on the most likely place in the crack and hammered it home, closing his mind to the misuse of tools as the iron hammer thumped on the wooden screwdriver handle. He levered hard against the frame and the panel stirred and scraped and moved grudgingly outward half an inch. Then it stuck and Septimus could feel the piece of slate trying to bend against the pressure of the screwdriver. He stopped levering before the panel snapped. Misusing the screwdriver as a chisel, he banged away at the point where the panel seemed to be jammed, then he started to lever again. He had to repeat the process three times, and so ruined his screwdriver, but at the third attempt the panel came free with a rush. He caught it just in time and laid it on a chair beside the tomb.

'What are you doing? Grave robbing?' It was Rosemary standing behind him. So engrossed had he been that he had not heard the opening of the door as she came into the Chapel.

'Just an idea,' he said. 'I was wondering where all the mice lived.'

He put a hand into the cavity beneath Sir John's pillow.

There was something there, something smooth and cool with corners. He put his other hand in and drew out a box. It was plain, made of untreated oak, still light in colour, almost as if the wood were freshly cut, because of all the years it had spent in darkness. It was held closed by a simple iron hasp with an oak peg thrust through it, and the box was heavy for its size. Septimus rested it on the top of the tomb.

'I think we've found Our Lady's Cup,' he said.

He pulled the peg from the hasp and opened the lid, the hinges squealing as he did so.

Inside, wrapped in red velvet, dry and brittle with age, was the Cup. The surprising thing about it, in comparison with the silver gilt replica, was its weight. Septimus took it from the red velvet and stood it on top of the tomb, six inches in front of the greedy eyes of Sir John. It was exactly the same in shape and decoration as the replica, but it was made of metal at least three times as thick, and because the metal was gold it was far more than three times as heavy. It stood there, gleaming dully, looking exactly as it must have done four hundred years earlier when it was put into the box and hidden away.

'There it is,' said Septimus. 'So that's what all those pilgrims came to worship. John of Danedyke hid it, Rosemary, and we've found it.'

'And I'll take it.' The voice was harsh and came from behind them. It was the bearded man who had driven the Jaguar, and he was standing ten feet away, between the communion rails, his back to the altar.

Septimus sighed. 'Yes, I suppose you will, Johnny.'

Several things had shot through his mind in the second before he spoke. First, as he turned, he had been aware of the hammer six inches from his hand. Second he had seen the gun in the man's hands, a gun that was all butt and breech, its twin barrels sawn off nine inches above the triggers. Had it not been for Rosemary, despite the sawn-off shotgun, he might still have risked it—thrown the hammer and dived for cover. As it was he let his hand slide from the edge of the tomb. Third— because of the shotgun—he knew who the man was. Edwin Bates—Buckshot Johnny.

Johnny spoke again, motioning with the gun. 'Put it in the box—slowly.'

Carefully Septimus did as he was told. He was still looking for chances, but was terribly aware of Rosemary beside him. Johnny with a gun in his hands was not to be trifled with.

Johnny came slowly toward them, the gun pointing, a finger on the trigger.

'You recognise me, copper. You didn't in Oxford.'

'It's the gun, Johnny. It jogs the memory. And you didn't have a beard in the old days.'

Johnny stood to one side and motioned with the gun toward the door leading out into the churchyard.

'I did ten years' bird because of you and Burroughs, and I'd as soon blow a hole in you as anything else. Open the door.'

Obediently Septimus went to the door, unlocked it and swung it open. The autumn twilight was blue across the church- yard. He stood, his hands at his sides, awaiting instructions.

'And you, Miss.'

Looking over his shoulder, Septimus could see the fear in Rosemary's eyes. He smiled at her, trying to give her courage.

'Do as the man says, Rosemary—on account of his popgun.'

He took her arm and they went out into the twilight with Johnny following ten paces behind, the gun hanging at his side.

11

Eggs and Bacon

Septimus helped Rosemary over the piece of fence at the Rectory end of the churchyard wall, while Johnny stood behind, watching them.

'Nice pair of legs you've got,' he said appreciatively.

Septimus took her arm again as they went across the field. He could feel that she was trembling.

'Don't worry,' he said, trying to give her courage. 'Last time he did ten years. He'll get another ten for this. He's a very stupid villain, is our Johnny.'

'What did you say?' Johnny's voice was harsh behind them.

Septimus did not reply. The hammers of the shotgun clicked as they came back.

'What did you say?'

'I said you were a very stupid villain, Johnny, And you'll soon be doing another ten years.'

'I'll fill you with buckshot before I do. I'd be glad of the excuse. So just watch it.'

The trouble was, thought Septimus as they stumbled along the hedgerow, Johnny was both stupid enough and violent enough to do exactly what he threatened. Johnny lived in a pre-adolescent world of cops and robbers. Bang! bang! and you're dead. And the trouble was that you might be—in terrible adult fact. Even so, had it not been for Rosemary, he might have risked something. But she did not belong to the grey world of prisons and crime, and he was not prepared to see her maimed or scarred for life. Not even for the sake of the

Cup . . . So with his arm through hers he led the way through the next field gate and into Danedyke Wood.

As Septimus had expected, the *Grace of Wisbech* was moored by the bank of the Danedyke.

Johnny stood above them with the gun and they scrambled down the bank and stood waiting on the deck.

'Now,' thought Septimus, 'now's my chance. He can't keep that gun at the ready while he comes aboard.' He relaxed his grip on the girl's arm and stood poised, waiting the moment. But it was not to be, Johnny was not that stupid.

'Go into the cabin and shut the door,' he said.

They did as they were bidden, sliding the door behind them, standing side by side in the dark cabin, saying nothing, listening for the thump of feet as Johnny landed on the deck.

The door opened.

'Copper. Have you got matches?'

'Yes,' said Septimus.

'There's a Tilley lamp hanging from the ceiling. Light it. And you, Miss, you can make yourself useful. There's a Calor stove behind you. The food's in the cupboard on the other side. Bacon and eggs and a tin of beans. My mate'll be here soon, and he'll be hungry, and so am I . . .' He slid the door shut.

Septimus put a hand up to the deckhead and groped for the lamp. He lit it at the third attempt, and its yellow light filled the little cabin.

There were seat beds on either side, a table folded up against the forward bulkhead. The galley was on one side of the door leading out into the cockpit, the food cupboard and a little sink opposite.

Septimus lit the gas while Rosemary took bacon, eggs and a tin of beans from the cupboard.

'Do you want to eat, Septimus?' she asked. He noticed the use of his Christian name. It seemed right in their dangerous situation.

'No,' he replied. 'I'm not hungry.' He was stooping down, peering into the cupboard under the cooker.

'Pity,' she said. 'Nor am I. Still, I might find a bad egg to fry for that horrible man. And I can leave the rind on the bacon.'

He smiled absently, not replying, his mind too busy. It would be highly dangerous and almost certainly futile to try to mix it with Johnny in the confined cabin, but there was a bag of tools in the cupboard. If he could incapacitate the cabin cruiser in some way, then Johnny and Ginger would be forced to make their escape over land—and that would not be easy with two prisoners. He dragged the tools out, turning them over, seeking for inspiration. There was a wheelbrace and a box of drills. Now that was a thought! He looked round the cabin. The windows over the bench seats were uncurtained, staring out on the night. He couldn't do anything about them. However, something might be done about the door. At least he could make it awkward to open.

Rosemary had begun to heat fat in the frying pan. She watched him curiously, but she said nothing, aware of the flimsiness of the door and the man standing in the dusk outside.

There was nothing he could do to jam the handle of the door. He crawled round Rosemary's legs, investigating the narrow space behind the cooker into which the door slid. There was a guide fixed to the bottom of it, which slid in a rail screwed to the deck. He tried wedging a screwdriver under the bottom corner of the door, but that would not work. There was a small hand saw which looked about the right length. He laid it cutting edge downward in the rail, its end against the edge of the door. There was a gap of about four inches between the saw handle and the side of the boat, and this he filled with a mallet. Theoretically the door was now jammed, but Septimus guessed that one would only have to push hard for the saw blade to bend and spring out of the channel. Still, it would provide some delay.

He turned his attention to the deck between the benches. The boards were fixed down with brass screws which fitted into little brass cups. Evidently they were intended for easy re-moval—which was what one would expect. He took the screws out of the two boards on the port side. Rosemary was frying bacon, watching him as she did so, the frying slice in her hand, her head turned. The sizzling from the pan concealed the small noises Septimus was making.

'How's that food getting on?' Johnny's voice came from outside, and they heard his footsteps on the deck.

Septimus shot down the length of the cabin, grabbed the frying slice from Rosemary, and dropped it with a clatter, shouting as he did so.

'Look out, Rosemary! Mind the hot fat.' He dropped to his knees between Rosemary and the door as the door handle started to move.

He slid the saw from the rail just in time. The door rasped down the side of the blade as it opened, and Septimus was kneeling in the doorway, his head on the level of Johnny's waist, talking brightly to cover the rasping noise.

'There's not much room in this galley, Johnny my lad. Don't open the door so suddenly. We nearly spilled the hot fat.' He held up the frying slice as if it was a tennis racquet.

Rosemary spoke with housewifely irritability.

'It's like trying to cook in a telephone kiosk. If you want something to eat, you just keep out of my way. Otherwise you can cook your own meal.'

Johnny stepped back a pace, watching suspiciously as Septimus struggled to his feet and gave the frying slice to Rosemary.

'You just get on with it,' he said.

'Supper in ten minutes,' said Septimus brightly, and slid the door shut again. He waited a moment and then re-inserted his makeshift wedge.

'What are you doing?' whispered Rosemary.

'You wait and see,' he replied, and went back to his planks.

They came out easily enough, and he peered down into the hole which smelt dankly of stale water. With his pencil torch he could see that there was quite a large area of the hull above the oily water in the bilge. He got the wheelbrace and a quarter inch twist drill from the toolkit. Rosemary, watching him as she broke eggs into the pan, suddenly realised what he was intending to do, and her whisper was a hiss of astonishment.

'You're not going to drill holes in the bottom?'

'Just watch me,' he whispered back, 'and make lots of loud frying noises.'

The drill went easily through the thin hull, and a satisfactory fountain of water followed it out of the hole. Crouching on the deck, Septimus looked at it with a little grin of triumph. There was another, unexpected noise above the sounds of frying, and Septimus suddenly realised that Rosemary was giggling. Squatting on his haunches he waved to her, and his lips formed the words 'Two minutes', then he stooped back over the gap in the planks. Now if he drilled a complete circle of holes and pushed the middle out . . . He suddenly thought incongruously of the sums he used to do at school. 'If a clergyman drills a hole of one inch diameter in the bottom of a thirty-foot cabin cruiser . . .' But at that moment there was a shouting outside in the darkness, two angry voices, and a thump on the deck.

Aware of the staring cabin windows and the bank of the Danedyke which commanded them, Septimus rolled over. Ginger had arrived and he was not going to be granted his two minutes, and the door handle was moving, and Rosemary was turning towards it, the frying pan in her hand.

The door budged, hesitated, and then slid open with a crash and a twanging noise as the saw jumped out of the rail. Then a lot more things happened all at once, but for Septimus they seemed to happen in slow motion, like an action replay on television, because he knew that he was very close to death.

The ugly barrels of the sawn-off shotgun came poking through the open door. They wavered, steadied, and pointed straight at him, the stubby barrels foreshortening to a little steel figure of eight lying on its side. And behind the figure of eight was Johnny, anger and hatred in his face as the yellow light of the Tilley lamp caught it. And beside Johnny was Ginger-whiskers yelping like a terrier beside a bull. And Septimus realised that whatever Gingerwhiskers might be shouting, Johnny was infallibly going to pull the triggers. He even had time to realise that his death would have very little to do with the Danedyke Cup or holes in the bottom of a hired cruiser. It was the slums and the 'nick', and the years of underprivilege and of smouldering hatred, and the whole unreal 'cops and robbers' world of the petty thug. Johnny had the chance to buck the system by doing a copper, and Septimus was lying on the floor under the barrels of his gun. Johnny pulled the triggers.

Even as he did so Rosemary brought the heavy frying pan swinging round like a table tennis bat. It hit the barrels of the shotgun as the cartridges exploded so that most of the charge went upward through the skylight and the rest of it carried the frying pan spinning into the cabin.

For a moment the cabin was filled with the roar of the explosion, and the air was full of powder smoke, flying glass, eggs, bacon, hot fat, and the whine of ricocheting pellets. Through it all Septimus saw the frying pan coming toward him, spinning in the air, like a great black football. He ducked, but too late. The frying pan hit him on the side of the head, and he passed from consciousness in a glory of exploding stars.

Septimus struggled muzzily up the hill into consciousness. He opened his eyes slowly and closed them quickly because of the glare of light which made his head ache even more. He was sitting up and his hands were behind his back. He tried to move them to feel his aching head, but they appeared to be stuck, and that was very odd.

He remembered that the pain in the back of his neck was the blow he had received in the darkness outside the Relic Chapel. That blow had been struck by a man called Edwin Bates, but he could not remember how long ago. Edwin Bates—Buckshot Johnny. He remembered the events of the evening and the frying pan coming flying toward him.

He opened his eyes again, slowly this time, ready for the

stab of pain. The cabin was a wreck, the skylight and two of the windows smashed, the upholstery cut by flying glass, and little attempt had been made to clear up. The floorboards had been replaced, but the place was littered with broken glass, and there was a fried egg lying on the bench opposite, its yolk congealing in a yellow streak down the side of the cushion.

Rosemary was sitting beside him. Her hands were also behind her back and her face was white and strained, but she had seen his eyes flutter open and managed to smile at him.

'Hello,' she said, 'I'm glad to see you again. I'm sorry I crowned you with the frying pan.'

'Don't mention it,' he replied, remembering the sinister figure of eight as the gun barrels had come down toward him. 'Just as well you did. Johnny would have shot me for sure. Paying off old scores.'

She shivered.

'He frightens me, that one. He's like a mad dog on a chain. The other one—Ginger—he's the boss. But he's not very well in charge. I think he's frightened as well.'

'I take it they plugged my leak?'

'Yes. Ginger did it with pieces of a pencil. Johnny held me while they did it . . .' She shivered again. 'Then they tied us up.'

'Where are they now?'

'They went out on deck. Johnny asked—something about a rendezvous. Then they went out. I don't think Ginger wanted me to hear.'

Septimus considered this piece of information, his mind beginning to work again despite the pain in his head.

'They actually used the word "rendezvous"?'

'Yes. Johnny said something like "What time is the rendezvous?" And Ginger looked at me, and then they went out on deck.'

Up to that moment Septimus had never really considered the *Grace of Wisbech* as anything but a base of operations, but the word 'rendezvous' suggested other possibilities. The cabin cruiser was certainly not a seagoing craft, but she would be safe enough inshore, and the Danedyke connected with the sea. It was a neat plan. Had things not gone wrong, the two thieves could have taken the Cup, delivered it to a seagoing craft at the mouth of the Danedyke, returned the cruiser to Joe Burton at first light and have been well on their way to London by the time the theft was discovered. Not that anyone would have known it was a theft—there would be merely the panel removed from the side of Sir John Carruthers' pillow, and nothing to tell what had been concealed there. And the Danedyke Cup would already have been on the high seas, and no one any the wiser. Come to that, the panel of the headrest could have been replaced and then probably no one would ever have known that anything unusual had happened.

Ruefully he began to recast his ideas about millionaire art collectors viewing stolen treasures in secret vaults. Getting hold of the Cup was not like stealing the Mona Lisa from the Louvre. Nobody had known it might still exist until Professor Hakenbaum had discovered the Danedyke Gospels.

The Cup could easily have been 'found' somewhere on the Continent, and it would be perfectly possible to forge a history for it. And the whole neat plan had foundered on Mary Crowle's determination and his own suspicious nature. But of course it had not foundered. It had succeeded up to a point. They had the Cup, although it was not yet out of the country, and they also had two prisoners—two prisoners who could identify Johnny and Ginger and swear to the identification in a court of law. And that was a very sinister thought indeed. A pair of thieves and a pair of prisoners, and in future there would only be room in England for one pair.

Perhaps Johnny had not been actuated entirely by hatred when he fired the shotgun. Johnny was stupid, but he was certainly a realist in the things he did understand. He would have about enough imagination to drop them both over the side. So a very great deal depended upon Ginger and the sort of villain he turned out to be. Also, if the whole business was not to end in tragedy he himself was going to have to play the end-game a great deal more skilfully than he had played the rest. He couldn't win now. He must play for a stalemate. But there the chess analogy broke down because of Rosemary. In chess you sacrificed the queen if necessary, but not in this game.

He looked sideways at Rosemary. Her hair was awry, and there were stains of grease across her blouse. Her eyes were big in her white face, but she managed to smile at him.

'Penny for 'em,' she said.

'At that moment, my dear, I was thinking about chess.'

12

Down the Danedyke

The sudden stammer of noise as the engine of the *Grace of Wisbech* came to life sent the seabirds clamouring in alarm across the dark Danedyke. Septimus and Rosemary felt the cabin cruiser tremble beneath them as her propellor began to revolve, and there was the sound of feet on the deck as her moorings were cast off, and the chuckle of water along her hull as she began to move toward the sea.

The door opened and Ginger came into the cabin. He was wearing a heavy blue duffel coat, its nautical air sorting ill with his little moustache and pointed, dachshund face.

'Ah. I see you've come round, as they say. Welcome aboard, Mr Treloar—or should I say back aboard, from your little journey to the Land of Nod?'

He simpered at a joke which Septimus quite failed to notice, since he was too busy working out his endgame.

'I'm thirsty,' he said, and his voice was something between a croak and a whine. 'Undo my hands for pity's sake and let me get a drink.'

Ginger sat on the bench opposite, and he was grinning so that Septimus really wanted to hit him.

'No,' he said. 'You're much too dangerous to untie. Trying to sink the boat! I'm surprised at you, Mr Treloar.'

Septimus licked dry lips with a dry tongue and simulated anger.

'Then get me a drink yourself, you ginger bastard. You owe it me. You've stolen my property, wrecked my church and killed my dog.' He watched the other man under lowered lids. It was an important moment—what he did not want was a drink supplied by Ginger. But he had so little to go on, he could only guess and hope to get the psychology right.

Ginger stiffened and the smile faded.

'I didn't mean to kill your dog,' he snapped. 'We only meant to take it away. But it attacked me, so I had to hit it. It was Johnny's idea anyway. I'm sorry about that. And I'm sorry about the damage to your church as well. That was another of Johnny's ideas. If I'd had my way we would have waited.'

Surprisingly, he really sounded as if he was sorry.

Please, 'whispered Septimus.' Please let Rosemary get me a drink.'

Ginger said nothing, but he pulled Rosemary to her feet and unbound her wrists.

'Get him a drink,' he said. 'And no funny business.'

Rosemary rubbed her wrists and stumbled down the cabin to the sink. She had been horrified by Septimus's sudden apparent collapse, and as she drew the water she felt more alone than she had ever felt in her life.

Septimus drank half the glass greedily, then he pushed it away with his lips.

'That's better,' he gasped. 'That's better. Rosemary, use the rest of it to bathe my face.' She did not wait for permission, for indeed, streaked as it was with dried blood, his face certainly needed bathing. She got out her handkerchief and set about the task without comment or permission from Ginger.

'And the back of my neck,' said Septimus.

She leaned forward obediently, the sodden handkerchief in her hand, her hair brushing his cheek, her ear close to his mouth.

'Rosemary,' he whispered. 'No, don't go tense. Keep bathing. When he ties your hands again clench your fists and keep your wrists apart.'

She said nothing, but as she stood upright she let her lips slide across his cheek in acknowledgement and gratitude.

She put the glass and the handkerchief into the sink and sat down again beside Septimus, her hands in her lap.

In the silence the three of them were aware of the puttering of the engine as the *Grace of Wisbech* went down the Danedyke toward the open sea.

Septimus was thinking that he had gained his first point, but the second was going to be much more difficult.

'That's better,' he said. 'Thank you, Rosemary.' And then after a pause, 'Ginger, what are you going to do with us?'

'Johnny and I were discussing that, and I must confess, we're not in agreement.'

'No,' said Septimus, 'I can imagine. You didn't bargain for murder when you took on the job of stealing the Cup, did you?' He spoke calmly, as if he was discussing the vagaries of the weather.

'Johnny says we should drop you overboard.'

'That's about Johnny's imaginative level. But you would still have a problem even then. That picture postcard I pressed on you in the church—the one you didn't take. I sent it to an old friend of mine at the Yard. You left a fine set of prints on it.'

110

'Still no problem,' said Ginger. 'My prints aren't on any police file.'

Septimus had expected the reply, but it had been worth a try.

'Ah. But Johnny's are. We got a good set of his from the broken water cruet in the chapel.' If the truth did not work, perhaps a lie might.

Ginger stopped smiling and his blue eyes were suddenly watchful.

'So?' he said.

'So if we disappear, it won't be a matter of country churches and local policemen. Once those prints are identified, it'll be a full-scale international manhunt—with you at the receiving end, Ginger. There's about six people who can identify you both. We know where this cruiser came from, and Scotland Yard has got fingerprints for both of you.' Septimus leaned forward to the other man, putting all the authority he could into his voice.

'If we disappear, you'll never come back to England, Ginger; and you'll never be safe in any country that has a police force. Sam Burroughs—Chief Inspector Burroughs—is my closest friend, Ginger. We worked together for twenty years and he knows as much as I do about this case. It was Sam and I who sent Johnny down last time . . .' He could see the doubt and fear in the pale eyes. 'No. You didn't know that. He didn't tell you, did he? But if we disappear . . . well, that's one case that Sam Burroughs won't let rest on the files. He'll hound you, Ginger. He'll hound you through every civilised country in the world.'

Ginger was now clearly frightened, and with sudden insight Septimus saw how little his brand of sophisticated villainy had prepared him for Johnny's bleak world of mindless violence.

'What have you in mind?' Ginger was whispering now. It was almost as if he was pleading, so complete was the reversal of roles.

Septimus ignored the question for the moment, turning the

screw tighter while the *Grace of Wisbech* sailed northward through the night.

'What are you and Johnny getting for the Cup, Ginger? Five thousand apiece . . .'

He deliberately put the figure far higher than he thought it would be.

'Not that much. But how far would five thousand go? Ten thousand, come to that. False names and obscure hotels and moving from country to country. And who's going to employ you in future, when the art theft world knows that Interpol are after you already for the last job you bungled in England? You won't even be able to turn a dishonest penny. You're finished, Ginger.'

He leaned back, waiting.

Rosemary gazed at him, fascinated. He looked old and grey and he still had streaks of blood across his face, and he needed a shave, and his tweed suit was torn and dirty and his clerical collar had come adrift at one side. But his big frame, mountainous in its stillness, dominated the quiet calm.

Ginger shifted his feet so that the broken glass crunched. Rosemary could see that one of his eyelids was quivering.

'What do you suggest?' he asked, and then again as Septimus remained silent, 'What do you suggest?' almost like a child asking an adult for advice.

'What do I suggest? I suggest you're in a mess, Ginger.'

The other man suddenly exploded into the anger of fear.

'It's that idiot Johnny! He's messed it up all along. He's a thug, nothing but a brainless thug. If we'd done it my way, you'd never even have known we were after the Cup.'

'True enough,' said Septimus gently. 'But you shouldn't tangle with people like Johnny. He plays with the rough boys, and it's a different game from yours. But I'll make a bargain with you. Who are we meeting out at sea?'

Ginger's eyes suddenly went cautious. 'I'm not telling you that,' he said. 'But it's a yacht. What's this bargain?'

'You leave the Cup with me. I'll let you and Johnny go

aboard the yacht, and I'll give you my word not to inform the police about the robbery.'

Ginger stared at him, his eyes round with surprise.

'Johnny'll never agree to that,' he said.

'That's your problem,' said Septimus harshly. 'But that's my offer, so you'd better see what you can do about persuading him.'

Ginger stood up. 'He'll never agree,' he said. 'I didn't realise until tonight how he hates you.' He turned to Rosemary. 'I'll have to tie you up, Miss.'

Hopefully she held out her wrists in front, but he made her turn so that he could tie them behind her back. She clenched her fists and tightened her muscles while Septimus talked in order to hold Ginger's attention.

'Your best bet with Johnny,' he said, 'is to get him to see that his own safety is at stake. Get that through his thick skull, Ginger, and you're home and dry. Of course I don't say it will be easy . . .'

When they were alone in the cabin Rosemary said, 'Do you think he will agree?'

'Not a chance,' said Septimus, 'so while they argue, we'd best do something about these ropes.'

The Tilley lamp was swinging gently overhead as the Dane-dyke widened and the *Grace of Wisbech* responded to the first premonitions of the open sea. From outside the cabin came the sounds of fierce argument.

Septimus and Rosemary sat back to back like a pair of ill-matched bookends and they set about extracting Rosemary's hands from the ropes. Instructed by Septimus, she put the heel of her left thumb into her right palm and tried to pull her left hand out of the ropes. Her body was arched backwards with the effort, and she was aching in places she never knew existed. The ropes were scraping like sandpaper across the backs of her hands, and Septimus was forcing the ropes downward with his fingers, his nails scraping on the pinched folds of her skin.

'You're killing me,' she said fiercely.

'No, I'm not. You're the first female Houdini.'

There was a final agony as the rope passed over her knuckles, and then with a rush her left hand came free. With a gasp of relief she eased her straining back and brought her hands round to the front. She slid the coils of rope from her right wrist and sat for a moment, chafing her wrists. Septimus smiled at her.

'There, I told you. Miss Houdini. You can make a living at it any time. Now undo me.'

The sounds of argument outside rose to a sudden crescendo as if Johnny and Ginger were about to come to blows. Septimus flapped his bound hands behind his back.

'Come on, Rosemary,' he said. 'We may not have much time.'

The knots were tight and it took her some time to unpick them and she broke three finger nails in the process.

He brought his hands from behind his back, rubbing his wrists as she had done, flexing his shoulders, sighing with relief at the absence of strain. He cocked an ear, listening to the grumble of voices, Ginger's treble and quick, Johnny's bass and slow.

'Now we tie ourselves up again. A real Houdini trick this time. Watch what I do.'

He took the rope and folded it in half, coiling the centre into a neat Catherine wheel which he grasped in his palm.

'You saw what I did?' he asked, looking at her pale face. She nodded, and he put his hands behind his back.

'Right. Now tie my wrists as tightly as you can.'

She did as she was bidden, pulling the reef knot as tight as she could.

'Good,' he said. 'Now we'll do the same for you.'

This was more difficult because once again Septimus had to work with his hands behind his back, and he had to do it without letting go of the coil of rope. It was a laborious business which brought the sweat to their brows, but at last it was done, although the knots were not as tight as Septimus could have wished.

So they rested, leaning back against the cabin side listening to the grumble of conversation.

The voices were suddenly cut off at a sharp word from Ginger. The steady note of the engine fell away and there was a gentle bump as the bows of the cruiser hit something solid.

Danedyke Number One, 'said Septimus, listening to the sounds outside, picturing someone jumping ashore to work the crankhandle of the lock in the darkness.' Danedyke Number One' was the last sluice and lock before the sea, a massive affair of oak boards. In terms of the fens it was the first line of defence against flooding. In terms of the *Grace of Wisbech* it was the last and heaviest of a series of lock gates, before the open sea.

There was a clanking from the dark shore as the sluice was operated, and then the cabin cruiser moved slowly forward again. Then there was another pause, more clanking and then a thump as someone landed on the deck and the engine settled on an even note. The cruiser surged forward, starting to rock now, setting the Tilley lamp swaying in earnest as she began to feel the sea reaching long fingers between the sand and mud-flats of the Wash. The cabin door slid open and Johnny stood in the doorway, his head stooped, his shoulders seeming to hold apart the doorposts. He was swaying with the new movement of the boat, and he had half a bottle of whisky in his hand.

'Bloody copper,' he said, 'I'm damned if I'll do it. I'll not part with the Cup. See you dead first, copper.' He came swaying into the cabin and stood between Rosemary and Septimus, looking first at one and then at the other.

'You'll be damned if you don't,' said Septimus evenly. 'You're drunk, Johnny, otherwise you'd see it. Spend the rest of your life doing bird. I thought you were smart, Johnny.'

Out of the corner of his eye Septimus could see Ginger at the wheel. His head was turned toward the cabin, his face was white and frightened. Johnny took a swig from the bottle, and then his hand came down on Rosemary's head and stroked across her cheek and down her breast.

'Little girl,' he said, 'pretty li'l girl. Like to take you with me.'

He turned to Septimus, reeling as the cruiser rose to the sea.

'Bloody dick. Drop the bloody dick overboard with concrete for boots.'

He took another drink and the whisky spilled down his chin and glistened on his black beard.

'Did for your tyke. Roughed up your chapel. Didn't we then, bloody dick? Teach you to send me down.' He sat with a bump, put the cork in the bottle, and was suddenly apparently sober.

'Treloar. Ex-Chief Inspector bloody Treloar. Tell you what, parson, I'll make a deal.' He rolled back the sleeve of his jacket and took a knife from the sheath strapped to his forearm, a wicked double-edged thing with a five-inch blade. He laid the knife on the bench beside him.

'There, copper. I'll leave it there. Rendezvous in thirty minutes.' He leaned forward and tapped Septimus on the knee. 'Here's the deal, bloody dick. We gag you two and turn out the light in the cabin. We abandon the boat, see? Then when we've gone you can cut yourselves free and get ashore. So you've lost nothing, have you then? But I take the Cup, and I want a promise. Otherwise I shall have to drop you both overboard, shan't I?'

'What promise?' asked Septimus.

'No Interpol. And you play it cool—so's we can get back into the country.' Despite the chilling knowledge that Ginger had failed and that Johnny was drunk and stupid enough to carry out his threat, Septimus was intrigued. 'But, Johnny, you wouldn't trust a copper to keep a promise like that, would you?'

'Ah. But you're not a copper now. You're a reverend. I'd trust a reverend even if he was a copper once. Haven't got much choice, have I? Nor have you—unless you want to be dropped overboard, and your girl friend.'

It was curious how, for all his stupidity, Johnny had read the situation correctly. Septimus knew that once he gave his word he would have to keep it.

'You don't leave me much option,' he said with a little sigh. 'Very well, Johnny, you take the Cup, and we go free and I'll not pursue the matter.'

'You promise as a reverend? You promise on the Bible?'

'Yes, I promise as a reverend.'

'That's all right then, innit?' said Johnny. He slid the knife back into its sheath, uncorked the whisky, took a swig and went out into the cockpit, shutting the door behind him.

Rosemary looked sidelong at Septimus.

'Are you going to trust him?' she asked, disbelief in her voice.

He shook his head. 'No more than I'd trust a delinquent five-year-old,' he replied. 'But we've got to play along. He really would drop us overboard, and I'm getting a bit long in the tooth for fighting Johnny.'

She shuddered violently.

'Like the kids in the playground,' she said. 'Bang! bang! and you're dead. And you would be as well.'

'Yes,' he said. 'Only he's cunning with it. There's more to Johnny's deal than he's told us yet.'

There was a sudden thump on the hull of the *Grace of Wisbech* and a spume of spray came through the broken cabin window wetting them both.

Here was another danger. At the back of his mind while he had been talking to Johnny, Septimus had been aware that the movement of the cabin cruiser had been getting steadily more lively. Now she was positively rolling, the lamp creaking on its hook, her scant timbers groaning with the unaccustomed strains to which they were being subjected. He began to won-der what rendezvous the two landlubber villains had arranged. 'Three miles off Hunstanton light' might sound well enough when you said it in a Wisbech telephone kiosk. It might be an altogether different matter in the wide waters of the Wash in the middle of the night with a stiff breeze blowing from the north-east.

There was another thump as a wave hit the frail side of the hull and more water came through the broken window and Rosemary was thrown hard against his shoulder.

'Johnny!' yelled Septimus. 'You'd better get her bows into the wind if you want to keep your rendezvous.'

There was no reply, but the lively motion eased, so he could only guess that they had taken his advice.

The engine revolutions fell away and for five crawling minutes they rode quite easily, the cruiser lifting to the waves, the sea noisy as it hissed down the hull.

'There she is!' It was Ginger shouting, his voice clear in the cabin, despite the sounds of the sea.

Septimus turned awkwardly on the bench and thrust his head dangerously out of the broken window. The breeze was cold on his face, there was no moon, and the horizon was dim under a few stars. Far away on their port quarter a light was winking. Septimus read the morse out loud. A . . . D . . . G . . . endlessly repeated. It meant nothing to him, but it was obviously a recognition signal.

13

The Open Sea

Rosemary knelt beside Septimus and together they watched the endlessly repeated signal. The engine note rose again and the *Grace of Wisbech* turned, sending the signal light sliding across the horizon as her bows came round. She started to roll again and there was a clattering over their heads, and a light stabbed out from the darkness of the cabin roof as their own signal lamp flickered in reply.

Whoever had operated the signal climbed down, there was a brief burst of conversation—inaudible because of the sea noises—then there was a sudden sharp cry, and then silence. Septimus tensed, knowing that something had happened in the darkness outside, not knowing what. He turned from the window, sat down and waited, and Rosemary followed his example.

The door slid open and Johnny appeared, framed by the night. He was stooping a little because he had a burden on his shoulders, and the burden was an unconscious Ginger.

Johnny was grinning triumphantly. He dropped his unconscious colleague on to the opposite seat and looked down at him.

'You stupid, college-educated git,' he said, 'I told you I wouldn't give up my share, didn't I? Now you've lost yours.'

The *Grace of Wisbech* rolled alarmingly, sending Johnny off balance, bringing gallons of water slopping into the cabin. With no one at the helm the cruiser was lying broadside to the sea.

'You'd better get back to the helm,' said Septimus calmly. 'Beam on, she'll capsize before long.' Despite the calmness of his speech, he was tense, expecting the wicked knife to be slid from its sheath, ready to throw himself sideways, ready to slide his hands from the useless bonds, ready to fight, knowing as he prepared himself that it would be a useless gesture, a fight he could not possibly win. But he must try for Rosemary's sake. Suddenly he thought incongruously of Sir Handel with bared teeth waiting in the Rectory kitchen. He did not suppose that dogs got to heaven, but if by any chance they did and could talk when they got there, he would have an interesting conversation with Sir Handel . . .

Johnny went. But not for his knife, for the tea towel which hung by the sink. He tore it in two and gagged Rosemary with one half and Septimus with the other. He checked the knots and their bonds, and tightened Rosemary's, and all the while the *Grace of Wisbech* rolled like a barrel in a millrace and the sea came crashing through the broken cabin window.

Septimus was fighting a desperate battle with himself. Now! While Johnny was stooping over, occupied with Rosemary's wrists, now he could slip his own bonds and attack. But he knew it would never do. Once he could have dealt with Johnny— but not now. That way lay certain death for both of them. And there was another way—if only he had the moral courage to hang on. He could see Rosemary's eyes as she looked at him over the top of the tight gag, and he closed his own eyes to shut out the temptation.

Johnny stood up, bracing himself with one hand against the cabin side, and stretched up with the other, turning off the Tilley lamp.

Just before the lamp hissed into darkness he looked at Rosemary.

'Sorry, Miss,' he said. 'But you shouldn't have mixed it with me.It's just hard luck—innit?' Then he looked at Septimus.

'Goodbye, copper. Think of the Scrubs while you're trying to undo them ropes.'

The cabin was dark and loud with the battering of the sea. Johnny went out into the night.

Septimus waited until the engine note rose and the bows of the cruiser came round to the sea, then he slipped his hands out of the rope and removed his gag. Rosemary copied him and they sat a moment rubbing their wrists.

The cruiser was riding more easily now, and Septimus stooped over the silent form of the unconscious Ginger. He dared not use his torch with Johnny so close outside the cabin door, but he passed his hands across Ginger's face and listened to his breathing.

'He'll be out for a bit yet,' he whispered. 'Johnny must have given him a tidy clout.'

'What now?' she asked, her face close to his in the darkness. 'Have we got to let him get away with the Cup?'

'No,' he replied, conscious that she was trembling. 'But we've got to play it carefully.'

So they stood together in the darkness of the wrecked cabin, the sea noises loud about them as he told her what he planned to do.

'So can you steer the boat?' he ended.

'Yes,' she said. 'I often do it for Tom when he's servicing a marine engine.'

'Good girl. You've got it clear?'

'Yes,' she said, 'I'll do exactly what you said.' He realised that she had stopped trembling.

The engine was suddenly throttled back and they heard Johnny shouting to the yacht.

'Not long now,' said Septimus. And then, 'We'd best sit down in case he comes into the cabin for a last look.'

He extracted a hammer from the toolkit and laid it on the bench beside Rosemary.

'If he decides to have another look at your ropes, hit him with that, and I'll be on his back quick as Christ'll let me.'

They replaced their gags, and waited, their hands behind their backs, while Johnny held the cruiser's head to the sea.

Suddenly there were voices close alongside, orders being called in a tongue which Septimus could not identify—Polish perhaps, or more likely one of the Scandinavian languages.

The door opened and Johnny came in. He took a quick look at Ginger with a torch, satisfying himself that he was still unconscious. He flashed the light briefly on the faces of his two prisoners and went out again without saying anything.

The engine of the *Grace of Wisbech* stopped, and Septimus felt the bump against the hull as the rowing boat from the yacht came alongside. There were one or two sharp orders in the unknown tongue, and then the noise of Johnny scrambling over the side of the cruiser, and then the splashing of oars as the boat pulled away.

Septimus waited a full thirty seconds, then he stood up, dragging the gag from his mouth and leaving it to hang round his neck.

'Right,' he said. 'Let's get cracking.'

After the gloom of the cabin it seemed light on the deck. There was no moon, but the clouds were blowing away and the sky was a great bowl of stars. There was a stiffish breeze, and once again the *Grace of Wisbech* was swinging beam on to the sea and beginning to roll alarmingly. The unknown yacht lay hove-to less than a hundred feet away, a long low seagoing craft with light blazing from cabin windows and portholes. The rowing boat was halfway back across the gap of heaving black water separating the two craft.

Septimus gave his pencil torch to Rosemary. She was more likely to need it sorting out the controls on an unknown engine. He went along the deck, hanging on to the handrail on the cabin roof because of the way the cruiser was rolling, sending the sea breaking over the deck, tugging with icy fingers at his legs.

The spotlight was on the forward extremity of the cabin roof, and as he heaved himself up beside it Septimus heard a shout from the yacht. It was answered from the boat and there was a sudden flurry of conversation across the narrowing gap of water. He guessed that someone had seen the pencil torch that Rosemary was using in the cockpit and was asking questions, but he did not understand the language being used, nor did he know what lies Johnny had told, neither did he greatly care. The lamp was beneath his hand and he was fumbling for the switch and the engine was coughing into life, and then the bows of the *Grace of Wisbech* were coming round toward the yacht and he was ready.

The rowing boat was alongside the yacht. It was brightly illuminated by a deck lamp. Someone was attaching the falls ready to haul it up, and Johnny was going up the ladder to the deck. Septimus could see him hanging on with one hand, the Cup in its box clutched under the other arm.

Septimus lay on the deck waiting, his hand resting on the switch as the *Grace of Wisbech* turned toward the yacht and the distance between the two boats diminished. There was more shouting from the yacht and he saw people come out of the darkened wheelhouse and cross the deck and lean on the rail, gazing across the narrowing strip of water. There was a loud hail, a sharp question called and repeated, but he ignored it.

Now the *Grace of Wisbech* was a mere twenty feet from the yacht and moving quickly toward the bows of the larger craft.

He trained the lamp round and switched it on, sending a sudden finger of white light stabbing across the dark sea, making a circle of blinding whiteness on the hull of the yacht . . . Septimus moved the lamp, sending the circle of light skating along the hull, lengthening into an oval as it moved forward. He adjusted the lamp, sending it hesitating, flickering over the bows.

There it was! Septimus steadied the light, training it on the flared peak. The name of the yacht picked out in gold letters. SS *Elsinore*.

He grinned in the darkness. Now he was going to win.

He brought the circle of light skimming back along the deck to the group of men at the rail by the wheelhouse. They were in white uniform, talking to one another, gazing down at the

Grace of Wisbech. He moved the light aft. Johnny was standing by the door to the main cabin talking to a man with grey hair. Johnny had the Cup under his arm.

He held the light steady and shouted more loudly than the distance warranted.

'SS *Elsinore*, ahoy!' A pause and then, 'SS *Elsinore*. Anybody aboard speak English apart from that burglar's apprentice Edwin Bates?'

There was an indefinable pause and then two voices spoke almost in unison. The first was a sharp command in the unknown tongue and it came from the white-uniformed group by the wheelhouse. The second was a shout from Johnny.

'Bloody copper. I ought to have knifed you while I had the chance.'

In response to the sharp command the gentle pulsation of the engines of the SS *Elsinore* rose to a roar and she started to draw away.

Septimus ignored Johnny.

'I shouldn't, Captain,' he shouted. 'I really shouldn't. SS *Elsinore* will be in Lloyd's Register. Your owner won't be pleased with you when the police arrive.'

The rumble of the engines fell away again and the *Grace of Wisbech* pulled alongside once more.

'That's better,' shouted Septimus. 'Now is there anyone who speaks English? Because I want that Cup back and I'm longing to tell someone why I'm going to have it.'

'I speak English.' The voice was quiet, with hardly a trace of accent. It was the grey-haired man standing beside Johnny. He came to the rail and stood in the glare of the spotlight as he spoke. As he moved, a much more powerful spotlight blazed out from the yacht, illuminating Septimus as he lay spread-eagled on the cabin roof. The voice of the grey-haired man came calmly out of the darkness.

'If we both extinguished our lights, Mr Treloar, conversation would be a great deal easier, I think.'

Septimus switched off the spot and a moment later the one

on the yacht went out. The darkness seemed absolute, but after a while the shapes of the two boats reasserted themselves, and Septimus could see the other man leaning on the rail, silhouetted against the lights of the cabin.

'Mr Olov Hellerstedt, I take it,' he said with all the nonchalance he could muster, and quoting the one likely name from Sam Burroughs' list. Now was there or was there not a second of hesitation before the grey-haired man replied?

'You can take it or not, as you please, Mr Treloar. I am holding up my voyage with a great curiosity to hear what you have to say to me.'

'No matter,' said Septimus. 'Hellerstedt's the name on the Interpol suspect list . . .' (He made it sound as sinister as he knew how), '. . . But even if you're not Hellerstedt, your boat will be in Lloyd's Register and I know you've got a valuable piece of stolen property aboard—my property so far as it's anyone's. What's more, the thief is standing behind you. At least one of them. We've got the other one aboard with us. He's unconscious, and no doubt the English police will be delighted to take him off my hands. That's why you're going to give me back the Cup, Mr Hellerstedt—even if your name isn't Mr Hellerstedt.'

The conversation which followed was a curious one, for Septimus knew that he possessed a cast-iron hand and the unknown man on the yacht betrayed no emotion at all. He argued coolly, as if it was an academic question, as if he was arguing for the sheer joy of the intellectual pursuit, and all the while the two boats rode side by side in the black night and the crew of the SS *Elsinore* stood on the deck and listened.

There could, as Septimus knew, be only one end to the argument. The successful theft of the Cup depended on secrecy, and that had been forfeited by the actions of Johnny and by the fact that Septimus knew the name of the yacht. The only alternative was murder, and the chance for that was past—even if murder figured in the plans of Mr Olov Hellerstedt—or whoever owned the yacht.

Septimus brought the conversation to a close.

'So we'll just pull alongside, Mr Hellerstedt. Then you can drop the Cup down to me, and we'll forget about the matter. I suggest you give Johnny a job sweeping the floor in one of your machine tool factories—but he'd better not come back to England. And when Ginger wakes up from the clout that Johnny gave him, we'll let him go with a caution . . . so long as he promises to be a good boy in future.'

'Ah, Mr Treloar, your urbanity does my sad heart much good. But can I trust your discretion? After all, what guarantee have I that you will not go straight to the nearest police constable with a tale of the most horrific? Or even worse, perhaps you will sell the biography of the whole regrettable episode to one of your Sunday newspapers.'

'Well, you've got my word, Mr Hellerstedt—for what it's worth. And apart from that you really haven't got much option, have you?'

'Look out, Septimus!'

It was a sudden shout from Rosemary, and as she shouted she opened the throttle of the cruiser, sending the *Grace of Wisbech* surging forward, throwing Septimus sprawling from his sitting position on the cabin roof.

A fraction of a second after Rosemary shouted there was a flash and the report of a gun from the deck of the yacht. By its lurid light, even as he fell over, Septimus saw Johnny standing behind Hellerstedt, the sawn-off shotgun to his shoulder. And as he saw it, so he felt the pluck of wind as the pellets passed him and a stab of pain in his shoulder as some of them went home and he tumbled across the deck.

'Are you all right, Septimus?' It was Rosemary calling anxiously as he picked himself up. He reassured her, saying nothing about his shoulder.

There was a scuffling and a shouting on the deck of the SS *Elsinore*, and then Hellerstedt's voice came out of the darkness, sharp with anxiety.

'Are you all right, Mr Treloar?'

'Yes,' said Septimus. 'Small thanks to that hired thug of yours.'

'He is being dealt with,' said Hellerstedt, his voice calmer now. 'I greatly regret that that should have happened. I must confess it never occurred to me that a servant of mine would do such a thing.'

Septimus suddenly thought of the proverb about the Devil and a long spoon, but he was too tired to quote it, and his shoulder was hurting like hell.

'No harm done,' he said. 'We'll come alongside now and you can drop the Cup down to me.'

He struggled to his feet on the heaving deck and waited while Rosemary brought the *Grace of Wisbech* alongside, realising as she did how fortunate he was that she was such an expert. It was just as well, because he himself was at the end of his tether, and Hellerstedt was leaning over the rail, the box in his hands and shouting something. And then suddenly the box was falling toward him and he was trying to catch it and discovering that he could only move one arm.

The box containing the Cup crashed to the deck and for a heartstopping moment slithered toward the sea. Somehow Septimus managed to stop it with his foot, and so Our Lady's Cup, the treasure which John of Danedyke had tried so hard to preserve, was not at the last moment lost in the Wash like King John's crown jewels.

Hellerstedt was still leaning over the rail.

'Hardly the way to treat Our Lady's Cup, Mr Treloar . . .' To Septimus the voice seemed to come from an infinite distance. It was bland, amused, grey with weariness.

'Now if it were mine . . . if the gods had so disposed the matter . . . it would receive the reverence it deserves.'

In the depths of his weariness Septimus was suddenly conscious of a great anger. This was the man. Mary Crowle had been attacked and Sir Handel was dead, and Rosemary had been in great danger, and Joe Burton's cabin cruiser was little short of a wreck, and his head ached and his arm was paralysed and he could feel the hot blood running down his wrist.

'Oh, get stuffed, you common sneak thief!' he said. Then he turned to Rosemary in the cockpit.

'Rosemary my dear, let's go home.'

Somehow he managed to remain standing on the cabin roof as the dark strip of water widened between the two boats. Hellerstedt stood leaning against the rail, motionless, silhouetted against the cabin lights, watching them go.

14

Homecoming

'But, Septimus, you can't send that letter! I mean . . . you're a clergyman. And that letter—it's . . . it's nothing but disguised blackmail.'

Septimus sat up in the hospital bed, his right arm still in a sling, and took the letter which she had written to his dictation. She was pink with astonishment, and wearing a white blouse and looking her most schoolmarmish and her most attractive, and Tom was sitting beside her, grinning and eating the grapes which they had brought with them on this visiting afternoon three days after the encounter with the SS *Elsinore*.

'Oh, can't I?' he said. 'You just watch, my girl. You type it, and I'll send it.' He looked at the letter. 'You'd be hard put to it to prove that was blackmail in a court of law.'

'Squire,' said Tom. 'You'd post a bomb to that Swedish character if you could get the Post Office to accept it.'

Septimus surveyed the younger man with cold blue eyes, remembering the world-weary silhouette on the deck of the SS *Elsinore*.

'Maybe I would at that,' he said, and turned to his letter, checking that he had said exactly what he wanted to say.

Dear Mr Hellerstedt,

It was a memorable experience for a country parson to meet you aboard the SS *Elsinore* the other day. What a beautiful yacht you have!

I was much encouraged by your sympathetic under-standing of our problems at St Mary's Danedyke, and greatly impressedby your intimate knowledge of our history. You will have seen from our English papers that the original Danedyke Cup has been found! Nobody more delighted than I!

It was actually concealed in the pillow of Sir John Carruthers' tomb, so your surmise that the thieves had missed it was quite correct.

I do congratulate you on the accuracy of your guess about the significance of the discovery by Professor Hakenbaum of the Danedyke Gospels.

Unfortunately—as you know—the thieves in their abor-tive search did considerable damage in our very beautiful Relic Chapel. The Diocesan Architect has made a quick preliminary estimate, and he reckons that it will cost no less than £500 to set all to rights, and unfortunately I can capitalize neither on the original Cup nor on the silver gilt replica. You will appreciate that both now rest secure in the bank, and the diocesan authorities will authorize the sale of neither the one nor the other.

Yes! I fear this is a begging letter. I am wondering whether I can move your generous heart to help us.

You will know from our conversation my own distaste for sensationalism, but £500 is a great deal of money for a small parish such as ours. As you can imagine, the discovery of the Cup and the attendant excitements have caused no small stir, and the journalists press me for what I believe is called 'the inside story'. In fact I was quite staggered by one representative of a Sunday paper who offered me no less than £1000 for an exclusive account! But I am not a sensationalist, and this is not my way. From my hospital bed I am already planning a fête and a bazaar to raise the money we need, and I have even been turning over in my mind the possibility of a Flower Festival, since these are the fashionable thing and can, I believe, be very profitable. But we should indeed be most grateful for any mite of financial support you felt moved to give us. Knowing your interest and great generosity I shall look forward to hearing from you.

Our mutual friend 'Ginger'—the architect, you will remember—sent his kind regards. He recovered from his migraine, and so after a long talk and with not a little hesitancy I let him go off to London. I think the job was too much for him as—rather to my surprise—I discovered that he had very little real experience. I think someone must have misled us both as to his qualifications. Anyway, I have agreed to keep a fatherly eye on him in future, and I think he should do very well.

My warmest regards to John. I so hope you will manage to find him a job in Sweden as I am sure your climate will suit him a great deal better than ours. From my pastoral experience of his complaint I am sure he will fare much better away from this misty island.

Yours sincerely,

Septimus Treloar.

PS.—Do come and see me at the Rectory should the SS *Elsinore* be off our coasts again. I will gladly arrange to show you the Cup.

He held the pencil-written sheets out with his left hand.

'An admirable document!' he said. 'You type it, my love, and post it to our square-headed friend.'

'You wicked old man,' she said, smiling and taking it from him. Then more seriously, 'Do you think we were wise to let Ginger go?'

'Yes,' he said cheerfully. 'He'll have to go straight, at least for a bit with Sam Burroughs breathing down his neck. He might even get an honest job. After all he has got a degree, and—you never know—he might find he enjoyed working for a living. Anyway if we ran him in, bang go our chances of getting Hellerstedt to contribute to the restoration fund.'

It was more than three weeks before Septimus received a reply to his letter, and he was home again, the wound in his shoulder almost healed. He sat at the breakfast table in the Rectory looking for a moment at the Swedish stamps, remembering the SS *Elsinore*, before he slit open the envelope. He smiled slightly as he read the short letter and then went to the study to ring Charles Simmonds. He dialled the first two figures of the doctor's number, and then paused, his fingers resting on the instrument.

No. Let them all wait. It would be more fun to make the announcement officially at the next meeting of the Parochial Church Council. That would teach Rosemary to call him a wicked old man.

The Council met on a blustery night in November. As always they sat at the end of the big schoolroom, close to the glowing coke stove, with Rosemary's sandtray pushed back against the wall out of the way. The room behind them seemed cavernous with its empty desks and diminutive tables, with its dolls house in one corner, its shop in another; with its walls covered with charts about the months of the year, multiplication, decimal coinage, and libellous pictures of the Rector taking a service in St Mary's. There were sinister jam jars on the window sills, and the wind rattled the tiles overhead, sending a fine film of dust falling from the rafters.

The meeting took its usual, predictable course, as inevitable as the procession of the seasons over the fens. As Tom Barton had once said, 'I don't know why we don't tape the meeting, Squire. We could leave it playing in the school and all go across to the Bluebell for a pint.'

Mary Crowle read the minutes of the last meeting, making them sound like an account of a school visit to Ely Cathedral. 'And a good time was had by all,' said Septimus when she had finished—but he said it under his breath. There were no matters arising. There never were.

Then Colonel Carruthers, the treasurer, delivered the accounts, standing very erect, his red face and white moustache raised, as if he was addressing a parade. He peppered the room with figures, like the random firing of an automatic weapon— very military and very efficient, and the accounts were in as parlous a state as ever.

Then they talked about the Christmas Bazaar, and Harry Garner—his arm still in a sling—held forth about the Mile of Pennies.

Then they discussed the Nativity Play, and Rosemary agreed to produce it yet again. Then they talked about the maintenance of the rotor scythe, and Tom Barton agreed to do that yet again. But not before he had had a passage of arms with his fellow churchwarden. Harry Garner remarked sourly that the church rotor scythe seemed to need more maintenance than the Home Farm tractors. To which Tom replied with some asperity that if Harry ever used the scythe—which was part of his business as warden—he'd know more about it, and if they spent a bit more time and money on the maintenance of the Home Farm tractors they wouldn't be such clapped-out heaps of old scrap iron. Harry was disposed to resent this, so Septimus butted in to prevent the meeting degenerating into a brawl. He quietened Harry to a glum mutter and took the meeting on to the last item on the agenda—the repairs to the Relic Chapel.

He read the report of the Diocesan Architect, which was not quite as bad as the original rough estimate. But it was bad enough for a tiny country parish. They needed no less than four hundred and fifty pounds.

The Colonel snorted, lumbered to his feet, and went off like a land mine. The building fund was seventy four pounds eleven shillings and fourpence in the red, and there was the appeal for the bells and the tower. And what was more, he took the strongest exception to the damage to the tomb of his ancestor, and what were the police doing about apprehending the criminals? There was now so much senseless vandalism and violence by young people. And what were the courts doing about it? It was really high time corporal punishment was brought back.

Then Mary Crowle said that she didn't know how Colonel Carruthers knew the culprits were young people. It had not been a young person who had knocked her down—if her assailant had anything to do with the damage in the Chapel, as she supposed he did. And anyway in her long experience with children she had come to the conclusion that corporal punishment—apart from a quick smack at the time—never did anybody any good.

Then the Colonel went redder in the face, and said that the cane had never done him any harm when he was at school, and blew through his moustache and made a noise which sounded uncommonly like 'Tchah!'

Then Harry Garner piped up, having got over his sulks and said that they would have to have a fête to raise the money. Harry liked fêtes as he was Danedyke's expert at bowling for the pig. And Rosemary sighed, knowing that if there was a fête she and Mary Crowle would have to look after the teas.

Septimus let them wrangle for a while, enjoying the predictable discussion, realising with a little glow of astonishment how fond he was becoming of them all.

At last he brought it to an end.

'Fortunately,' he said loudly, cutting across Harry Garner, who was well launched on sideshows, 'fortunately, none of this will be necessary. We've been given a cheque by a well-wisher. A Swedish gentleman who has a great interest in Danedyke and a collector's enthusiasm about the Cup . . .' Stony-faced he gazed over the table at Rosemary, challenging her to comment if she dared. Out of the corner of his eye he saw Tom start to grin, and he went on hastily in case Tom should say something indiscreet.

'Let me read you his letter,' he said.

'Dear Mr Treloar,

'I was most interested in all that you tell me about the Danedyke Cup. As you know, early gold and silver have been a lifelong interest of mine, and I can only say how glad I am that the famous Danedyke Cup has at last come to light, although I must confess it saddens me not a little to think of it languishing in a bank vault. It will be as invisible there as it was when it was concealed in the tomb, and I can think of many places where it would be more cherished and equally safe.

'I do agree, however, that untoward publicity does not agree with your calling as a pastor. I am able to share your revulsion as I am myself no lover of the limelight.

'To render it totally unnecessary, please accept the enclosed cheque as a token of my concern.

'I was glad to hear of the arrangements you made for our mutual friend the architect. I fear I was sadly mistaken in him.

'I have arranged a post for John in one of our plants up

north. I think it should suit his complaint as it is within the arctic circle. He sent his wishes to you.

'Yours sincerely,

'Olov Hellerstedt.'

Septimus looked up from his reading, savouring the expression on Rosemary's face.

'The cheque was for a thousand pounds,' he said gently. 'I must have paid it into the bank after you made up the accounts, Colonel.'

'God bless my soul!' said Colonel Carruthers.

'So we can repair the Chapel without holding a fête,' said Septimus.

'Aye, Rector,' said Harry Garner, a grin on his lugubrious face. 'And we can do the bells as well with a thousand quid.'

Septimus closed the meeting with a prayer, resisting the temptation to pray for Mr Hellerstedt in case he made Rosemary giggle.

In the post-prayer silence as they all stood among the infant desks and tables, their heads still bowed, Tom Barton said, 'We want you to come across to the Bluebell, Rector, now the meeting's over.'

'What on earth for?' Septimus asked in some surprise. Meetings of the Parochial Church Council often ended in the Bluebell, at least so far as the masculine part of the Council was concerned. But not, as it were, officially. They refused to tell him what it was about, and they trooped together across the road through the blustery night, chattering excitedly about the thousand pounds.

The bar of the Bluebell was fairly full, but in the little snug there was only Charles Simmonds waiting for the meeting to finish. There a babble of conversation as drinks were bought, and then Tom Barton slapped on the bar for silence, Septimus noticed that Mary Crowle had vanished through the door to the living quarters of the pub.

'Ladies and gentlemen,' said Tom. 'I've got to make the

speech because I'm Vicar's warden. I'm not one for speeches so I tried to persuade Harry to do it, but he said he couldn't. And the Colonel wouldn't because he said it was my job, and anyway if he started to make a church speech it would be bound to come out in the red, because his speeches always did . . .'

The Colonel clapped his hands at this.

'Not now, my boy,' he said. 'Not now.' And everyone cheered.

'Yes. Well . . .' said Tom, 'so I got the job. Well. Now everyone knows we've got a good Rector. Even if he hasn't been with us long. And even if he was daft enough to make me Vicar's Warden. And even if he was a copper once, so I have to keep my sticky fingers out of the collection. But the point is . . . we all know about the damage to the Chapel . . . And because he was a copper, the Rector did a bit of detecting, and went and found the original Danedyke Cup. It's a great help in the Ministry, having been a copper once. Every clergyman ought to have the experience. Because now we've got the Cup. In fact we've got two Cups. And although I didn't know it when I composed this speech, we've got a thousand pounds as well. . . so Harry Garner won't have to look after the Mile of Pennies after all . . .'

There was laughter, and cheers and 'Hear, hear's' so that Tom had to hold up his hands for silence.

'And if it wasn't for the Rector, we should have only one Cup, and a wrecked Chapel, and the Colonel's usual debit balance. So Rector, the Council clubbed together to make you a present.' He turned to the door by the bar. 'Come on, Mary, bring on the dancing girls.'

Mary Crowle came through the door with something clasped in her arms, something brindled and moving. She took it to Septimus and held it out as he struggled to his feet.

It was a Great Dane puppy.

'Here, Rector,' she said. 'With our love. We were all so sad about Sir Handel.'

He took the puppy in his arms, and it licked his face. He was too moved to say anything for quite some time. Then he stammered his thanks. And after that there was an awkward pause broken at last by the Colonel, whose training told him it was high time someone said something to help the Rector.

'Well, Rector, what are you going to call him?'

'It's not a him, it's a her,' said Mary Crowle. That brought laughter and an easing of the emotional tension.

Septimus looked round at them all: Mary Crowle . . . Charles Simmonds . . . Tom Barton . . . and finally his eyes rested on Rosemary.

'I shall call her Grace,' he said, 'Grace of Wisbech.'